F.W.B.

in gratitude

LAURA

a novel by

G.M.T. PARSONS

ST. MARTIN'S PRESS
NEW YORK

St. Martin's Press, Inc., 175 Fifth Ave., New York, N.Y. 10010

Printed in Great Britain

Library of Congress Catalog Card Number: 77-99122

First published in the United States of America in 1978

ISBN 0-312-47520-9

CHAPTER I

THE first severity of mourning was over. Mrs Young had returned thanks for the many kind letters of condolence, and callers in regular succession now began to appear at the house. The Youngs had lived only two years in Norwood and during that time had entertained very little, but they had been ushered into the neighbourhood by numerous introductions, and rumours of a fortune inherited in unusual circumstances aroused the curiosity of acquaintances as well as friends.

Laura and Nell, who in the ordinary way would have tried to avoid their aunt's visitors, found themselves better entertained than usual by drawing-room conversation. They too had benefited under their grandfather's will and they enjoyed the novelty of being styled heiresses, though they were contemptuously observant of changes in deference from friends.

'But after all money does count,' remarked Nell. 'I daresay we shall alter now that we are rich.'

'Well, I don't mind people who are respectful to us as much as I mind people who try to sympathize. That silly Mrs French yesterday spoke in such a gentle way, as if she expected us to burst into tears. And everybody knows we had never even seen Grandfather.'

'I find it all very interesting. One learns about human nature,' said Nell sententiously, staring at herself in the looking-glass, a habit of which her sister could never cure her.

'And we also learn far more about Uncle's plans than Aunt Carrie would ever tell us,' she added more briskly as she turned to follow her sister downstairs.

This was true. Mrs Young disliked imparting information about any but the most trivial affairs. She had imagined in girlhood that she was making an important marriage, and the illusion persisted after twenty-five years. She often perplexed strangers by speaking as if her husband's name must be known to them, and in the family circle she made a mystery of his comings and goings and insisted on referring even the smallest matters to him. 'I am not sure your uncle would like it,' she would say, or 'We must see if dear Uncle approves,' 'I would rather your uncle told you, my dear,' 'I cannot say till he comes.'

And since the settlement of the estate kept the master of the house constantly in Norfolk, the girls had been living more often than usual lately on this unsatisfactory fare. They listened therefore with the greater glee as their aunt, tentatively but firmly worked upon by visitors, betrayed detail after detail of their grandfather's illness and death and of the disposition of his property.

They were amused to watch the struggle of wills. Aunt Carrie did not mean to tell too much, and Miss Simpson, inquisitive but unsubtle, got a veiled snubbing and heard nothing at all. Mrs French hid a keen curiosity under a show of sympathy and found out nearly all she wanted to know. But today Mrs Woods was neither curious nor sympathetic. Death was death to her and money money, and she asked outright if the Youngs had decided to leave Norwood.

Aunt Carrie looked alarmed at the directness of the question.

'I think we shall move,' she said, 'perhaps in March. Dr Brown knows Norfolk and recommends the air for me.'

'And the girls go too?' Mrs Woods turned and smiled at them. She was fond of them and her daughter was their friend. 'Nell will come out this winter, I suppose.'

'Yes; her uncle thought of the county ball. And he means to give a dance at the Lodge as soon as the mourning is over.

The drawing room has a beautiful floor. Your Alice and Grace must come and stay with us.'

'How kind of you,' said Mrs Woods. 'They will be delighted. They have heard of the house, of course, from the girls. But is it possible,' she added, 'you have none of you seen it?'

Mrs Young shook her head.

'My father-in-law was most eccentric. After his wife's death – his second wife, you know, – he would never receive ladies. My husband says he once turned back a close friend who was arriving with his family to call. And he actually left instructions in his will that no women should be allowed to attend his funeral.'

'Very strange.' Mrs Woods sat plunged in thought. 'But what about the servants?'

'Men are always inconsistent,' complained Mrs Young. 'He kept on the housekeeper and all the maids who had been there when his wife died. Such an old-fashioned set, long past work, most of them. I am glad to say he left money for them to be pensioned off. I mean to take my servants with me when I go.'

'Well, it certainly sounds most romantic. But we shall be sorry to lose you.'

'It is good of you to say so.'

'And Grace will miss Laura particularly at the painting classes. She always says she learns more from Lolly than from poor little Mr Woodward.'

Laura flushed and Mrs Young made a deprecating murmur.

'Grace paints so prettily,' she said.

'Ah, yes, prettily; but Laura has real talent. You mustn't give up painting lessons when you move into the country, my dear.'

'Oh no, I never mean to,' Laura broke out. 'Never.'

'Of course she must go on with her painting, but I hope she will take more outdoor exercise. All this craning over an easel makes her poke.'

Mrs Woods laughed and turned the conversation, and Laura subsided into her own thoughts. She wished she could slip away with Nell and discuss the news they had just heard. They had telegraphed to each other their excitement at the discovery, but now Nell seemed to be absorbed in talk with the others and Laura was left to wonder if she would be sorry to leave Norwood.

Another move, she thought; Aunt Carrie was always moving. Three years in Cheltenham, then that horrid time in Bath; two years here in Norwood in a furnished house. Laura decided she would be sorry to go. She liked living on a hill, she like the big garden, and she had always liked the furniture and the wallpapers. 'Too aesthetic for me,' her uncle said, and he laughed at the peacock-feather pattern in the drawing room. Its blue-green was dismal in a fog, of course, but today in the bright February sunshine the room had begun to look as it did in the summer, like a sea cave, the iridescence on the paper making the walls seem aqueous. And Laura felt a sudden regret that she had never painted Nell sitting as now in the drawing room with the peacock feathers as a background and a green-blue light on her hair. 'Why do you choose such difficult subjects?' Mr Woodward always said. 'Miss Young, you go about looking for trouble.' He really liked Grace Woods better as a pupil: Laura's queer attempts perplexed him. But her problems and questions kept the class alert, and Grace Woods, sensible and straightforward like her mother, acknowledged Laura's superiority. The thought of leaving the drawing classes saddened Laura; she would miss them so much.

Still, Norfolk might be exciting. She and Nell flew to their bedrooms as soon as they could escape. Miss Bird was in the schoolroom; it was no good going in there. They were accustomed however to using their bedrooms as a refuge from the almost constant companionship of governess and aunt. They seldom slept together, the houses their uncle rented were too spacious for that; but they rarely had a sitting room of their own. Therefore all planning, quarrelling, or intimate conversation took place upstairs in the privacy of a bedroom. The times of putting on coats and hats, of changing for dinner, and the few minutes before lunch and tea when they washed their hands became occasions of unusual importance. Laura would save up questions to put while Nell was dressing, Nell would come in to chatter while her sister was brushing her hair. Tonight they sat together on Laura's bed and pulled a shawl round them, as the room was cold. 'Orphans,' said Nell, snuggling up to Laura. Then they swung their legs in unison and talked of the future. Not a shadow of regret was lurking in Nell's mind.

'Oh Lolly, I'm certain you'll like it when we get there. Think of a house in the country; it will be like living with Grandmamma again. And I hope we shall stay there till we are married; I'm tired of all this moving and moving, though it's worse for you than for me.'

'Why worse for me?' asked Laura in surprise.

'You make friends and then you have to leave them. You are really much more sociable than I am.'

'Oh Nell, you know how I hate parties.'

'And I love them. Oh well, I don't know. You like single people, I suppose, and I like them in crowds.'

Then a thought struck her.

'Lolly,' she whispered mischievously, her lips close to her sister's ear, 'Lolly, what d'you think will happen to Birdie?'

'Oh, she'll come with us.'

'Yes; but shall we have to share a sitting room with her?'

Laura looked troubled.

'We mustn't hurt her feelings. You know how easily she gets put out.'

That was always the difficulty; poor Birdie was so affectionate. 'I like making a niche for myself,' was one of her remarks. And in all their moves there had been Miss Bird's corner in the schoolroom, her uncomfortable desk with her pencil box on it, Laura's annual calendar pinned to the wall above, the chair with the cross-stitch cushion worked by Nell. Birdie never threw away anything that was given her; she had a tireless sense of gratitude and an infinite capacity for treasuring.

And Birdie had also made a niche for herself in the running of the house. Mrs Young had engaged her seven years ago when the death of their maternal grandmother left her nieces without a home. Birdie had taught Nell to the best of her ability, grinding her successively in the multiplication table, simple arithmetic up to vulgar fractions, the books of the Bible, the dates of the kings of England, the capitals and counties of the British Isles and then the capitals of Europe, the configuration of the world and its chief products, and nearly every irregular French verb.

But Laura had been another matter. Laura, five years older than Nell, had already spent a term at school. 'And schools may teach Euclid,' said Birdie, 'but they neglect good manners.' After a term's struggle she offered to resign her post. 'I can't manage her,' she complained. 'She does nothing but ask questions. She can learn if she likes, but she just will not learn my way.'

'But Miss Bird,' wailed Mrs Young, 'you are so successful with Nell. Her uncle is delighted with her progress.'

'Nell is easier. Laura, if I may say so, is very, very difficult.'

The difficult Laura was summoned by her uncle. She expected a scolding; she found him surprisingly mild.

'Explain to me what you dislike in Miss Bird's methods,' he said. 'She seems to me to be a painstaking teacher.'

'Oh Uncle,' Laura twisted her hands together in her effort to explain. 'She's so dull. Reasons don't interest her, you see. The governess at school could explain exactly why you do everything you have to do in arithmetic. Miss Bird just says "Turn the fraction upside down", and she doesn't know why and she doesn't really care.'

'But Miss Bird says you are backward in mathematics.'

Laura blushed.

'I don't try very hard. And I'm dreadfully untidy. Birdie says everything's bad if it's not neat.'

The result of this conversation was a change in the curriculum. A master (they were then at Cheltenham) came to teach Laura arithmetic, and an ugly little woman for French conversation. The subsequent move to Bath put an end to these hours and by the time they reached Norwood Laura was too old for lessons. But a recollection of the early days still divided her from Birdie; Nell was Miss Bird's child, Laura had been too difficult. Yet the course of their lives still kept them together, for by the time Nell's education was over Miss Bird had become more than a governess. With only one pupil to teach she had occupied herself in the house. She enjoyed arranging flowers, she liked running errands, by and by she offered to help with the accounts. From these she soon passed to housekeeping and Mrs Young slipped more and more comfortably into the position of cherished invalid with Miss Bird as a devoted slave to run affairs for her. Her husband accepted an arrangement that kept his wife happy and himself at ease; 'There must be no question of your leaving us,' he said. So Miss Bird passed her days in a frenzy of grateful activities, getting up early to rouse the maids, knocking on the girls' doors late at night if they were still burning candles. The sound of her footsteps as she pattered down in the morning or crept cautiously up to bed after making a last round always stirred a vague resentment in Laura and Nell. Birdie was so much more grateful than they were for the shelter of a home.

It was plain that the little governess would remain an inmate of the house, equally plain to the sisters that they no longer wanted her. Nell believed her uncle had begun to realize this; she told Laura she would ask him for a sitting room to themselves.

Her chance to do so came sooner than she expected, for when the girls went into the drawing room that evening before dinner they found that Mr Young was back from Norfolk. He was standing on the hearth rug with his back to the fire, a man of medium height with bright blue eyes and hair so black and plentiful that it looked like a wig. He had a pleasant voice and a charming smile.

'So we've heard the latest news,' he cried, as the girls came in. 'Well, what do we think?'

Laura paused, wondering which of her thoughts could be most safely expressed. Nell, as often, covered the pause by speaking.

'Oh Uncle,' she cried, 'we are so pleased.'

'You are? You are? Good,' he exclaimed, beaming at her. 'Well, we shall leave this house as soon as possible.'

And he took their arms to lead them into the dining room behind his wife with an impartiality so scrupulous that it was almost convincing. Affection shown to Laura was a sign of high good humour.

'Yes,' he said as he spread his table napkin, 'I think I have settled everything at last. If you can spare Miss Bird, my dear, for a day or two next week, I will take her down with me and show her round. She can go through the linen and speak to the maids. Then if she comes back and helps you pack up here we ought to be out well before the end of the month.'

'Everything is in good order?' enquired his wife placidly.

'Apple-pie order, wonderful. Poor old Mrs Duffin was an excellent housekeeper: she made a religion of her tasks. You don't find many of her sort nowadays.' And he leant back in his chair as a signal to the maids.

'Do tell us more about the house,' urged Nell; and her uncle, pleased, described Yule Lodge in detail, with its long approach through the park, its lawns, its shrubberies, the flower gardens, the handsome stone portico, the lofty hall lighted by a dome of glass, the pretty drawing room, long dining room hung with pictures, the morning room and the conservatory, and then the bedrooms upstairs opening on a gallery round two sides of the hall. 'A well planned house, not a bit too big, but convenient. Miss Bird will enjoy undertaking the duties of housekeeper.'

Dinner was over; the servants had left the room; the recital had lasted until dessert. Nell looked across at her sister and asked the important question.

'I have thought of that,' said Mr Young with decision. 'Miss Bird's new room is a very pleasant one, warm and sunny. I imagine she will like to have her desk in there. Besides, there will not be much space for her elsewhere. Your sitting room, I am afraid, is rather smaller than you have been accustomed to, but after all you do not need it as a schoolroom now, and your piano and Lolly's easel will fit in very well. You will be not disappointed, I think. By the way,' he added as the ladies rose, 'am I right, Laura, in supposing that your favourite colour is pink while Nell's is blue?'

Laura smiled and nodded, and Nell interposed. 'And am I right, Uncle, in supposing that you are planning one of your famous surprises – everything remembered, every detail perfect?' She laughed up at him as he held the door.

'You may suppose what you like, miss,' he retorted, pinching her ear, 'but you shall not get a word more on the subject out of me.'

The girls went early to bed. Laura, coming up first, looked into Nell's room and found the big cat on the bed. He was licking a back leg and he paused, leg in air, to glare at her as she stood in the doorway. She knew from his expression that he was not sleepy; the housemaid had probably pushed him in by force. She went on into her own room through the connecting door, pulled her curtains back, drew up the blind and looked out. The moon was full, half hidden from her sight by a gable of the roof. Laura opened the window and craned out to get a better view. She stood there dreaming till she heard Nell come in next door, then wandered back, still lost in thought, to speak to her sister. Shah slipped by her in the doorway but she took no notice. Nell however felt a draught and looked at her suspiciously.

'Is your window open?'

'Yes. Oh, has he gone?' Laura darted back too late. The cat had disappeared.

Nell was unhooking the back of her dress.

'He'll never come in if there's a moon,' she said. 'I'm going to fetch him.'

When she had taken off dress, petticoat and stockings she put on an old pair of shoes and buckled a voluminous ulster round her. Laura watched these preparations without disturbance; though she could not climb with Nell's agility she had herself followed Shah to the roof of the house and knew that the way from the ornamental balcony outside their windows to the outhouse at the back would be almost as easy for Nell as for a cat. If Shah had jumped down to the outhouse, Nell could not catch him; but the chances were that he would stop to play on the tiles.

Nell climbed out on the balcony, then Laura heard the ulster scrape the edge of the gutter and presently feet padded along the waterway running across the roof. At last the feet padded back again and Laura went to help.

'Here he is, very sulky,' said Nell from the roof, and Shah's reluctant body was lowered into her arms.

Laura nursed him while Nell jumped down and shut the window, and then washed her black hands and emptied away the betraying water, hollowed a place on her bed and spread a shawl for the cat. They put him down and petted him till the fierce look left his face and his body relaxed. But though he shut his eyes and purred stertorously he was by no means settled. Just as she fell asleep Laura heard her sister get up again, and she knew that Shah was insisting on his right to go out.

CHAPTER II

LAURA did not forget her scheme for a new portrait of Nell. The house was becoming disturbed by the bustle of packing, but she found opportunities when nobody was about to slip into the drawing room and study colours and light, and she had two satisfactory days of painting while Birdie was away in Norfolk.

Mrs Young, cossetting a cold, refused visitors and dozed tranquilly in an armchair by the fire. Laura was therefore able to ensconse herself on the boards by the window, where she could neither be accused of spoiling the carpet with her paint nor of disarranging the furniture. Nell had seized the chance of Birdie's absence to borrow a Rhoda Broughton and was glad of the excuse it gave to sit still and read. She even consented to sit just as Laura wished – 'though I shall get up and go away if you make me look aesthetic, Lolly.'

Laura smiled without speaking, intent on her work. A smell of paint began to spread, but Aunt Carrie's sense was dulled. Her head fallen back, she gave a little snore from time to time, woke up and straightened herself, and then dozed off again. Nell read absorbedly, flushed in cheek. The sun shone, the peacock walls glistened, an hour and a half slid by and the afternoon waned. At last Mrs Young woke up and complained that the fire was low. Nell rang for more coal and then came to stand by her sister.

'Why, you've put green on my hair and just under my nose. That's not very pretty and I'm sure it's not aesthetic.'

'It looked all right when the light was stronger,' said Laura. 'You mustn't criticize till the picture's finished.'

But Birdie's return from Norfolk interrupted the sittings. The energetic little woman was amazed to find how little had been done in the house during her absence. Nell had neglected to turn out the schoolroom cupboards and Laura was actually adding to her paintings instead of going through the old ones and throwing some away. There was no sense, either, in going on with the portrait: the vans would come before it was dry and the paint would smear in packing.

Laura gave up in despair, but she still hankered to finish her picture and became so absent-minded that Birdie did nothing but scold. New responsibilities were certainly weighing heavily on Birdie. She made a great business of shouldering her crosses.

'What is the house like?' asked the girls.

'Very pleasant. Not too grand, for which I am thankful, as it will be hard enough to run, so far in the country away from shops. Three miles from a station and there's nothing to be had in the village. At least, there is a grocer, and I suppose we must deal with him for some things, but I shan't trust him.'

'But what does the house look like?'

'Oh well, it is hard to describe. It stands back from the road and the drive comes in a semi-circle from the gates. Mr Young tells me he has half a mile of gravel to keep.'

'Is it pretty in front?'

'Not really, to my mind. I wish your uncle would have the trees down, though indeed I wouldn't for the world let him know I said anything about them. It is none of my business. But trees close to the windows of a house are always unhealthy; and your room and mine, Laura, look out into a sort of thicket just across the carriage sweep. Of course we shall be shaded from the heat in summer but anything so dark and damp at present you can't imagine. Still, one mustn't grumble. Mr Young is always so kind.'

Laura's heart sank but Nell cried eagerly: 'What are our rooms like, Birdie? Do give us just some idea.'

'Now, Nell, you know already it is no good asking me. If there is one thing I can do it is keep a secret. Your dear uncle wished me not to tell and I certainly do not mean to. In fact, I have better things to do than stay chattering here with you. And I fancy you yourselves could be employed. Mrs Young is sorting papers in the drawing room.'

Birdie bustled away, but the recollection of her words remained and weighed uncomfortably on Laura's spirits. After this whenever Yule Lodge was mentioned she saw an ugly house surrounded by trees, one wall blank like the wall of a prison, with two tiny windows set where the trees grew thickest. She knew this picture fantastic and yet could not forget it and began to be afraid of going away. She might have shaken off this depression if she could have escaped from Birdie, but a bad cold kept her strictly indoors where a half dismantled house gave little refuge. For two days she was hardly out of reach of Birdie's tongue. The continual fuss at last made both girls obstinate. 'If she comes in here again I shall leave the room,' said Nell. Laura felt too tired to speak.

On the morning of the move Laura woke with a start of terror and lay for a little while wondering where she was. The muslin curtains and the stuff ones had gone from her window and the daylight came in round an ugly green blind. Yet it was not for this that the window looked unfamiliar: it was smaller, less ornate than she expected it to be. She had been in another room facing another window, and there was something terrible about that room. She lay strangely oppressed by her broken recollections till she heard Nell moving about next door. Then in a flash she remembered the whole of the dream.

'Nell,' she called, and her sister appeared in the doorway. 'Nell, didn't I talk in my sleep last night?'

'My poor Lolly, I should think you did. You woke me up by your screaming and frightened me so that I came to see what was wrong. And there you were fast asleep, chattering all sorts of nonsense, and when I touched you you began to cry.'

'I think I remember your coming.'

'What was the matter?'

Laura frowned at the ceiling and tried to make out a connected story. She had been sitting or crouching by a door in the new house and Nell's face had appeared at the window of the room.

'I can't explain exactly why I felt so startled. Partly because we had just arrived at the new house and it is frightening to find something terrible in a strange place.'

'How do you know it was the new house?'

'I can't tell. It just was. It had a stone porch and a curved drive as Birdie said, and as we arrived someone made a joke and the horses jingled their bits. You know how in a dream you can be in two places at once? Well, I was in the porch arriving and I was upstairs listening to the horses. And suddenly I saw your face peeping in at the window. You weren't standing on the sill, you were craning round the corner. And it was so dreadful to see you there that I screamed and screamed.'

'Was it my face that frightened you?' asked Nell, gratified to be the source of so much agitation.

'No; something far more complicated than that.' Laura frowned and clasped her head. 'There was some great terrible meaning in the dream, and I understood it for a moment while I was asleep and I think I still understood it just now when I woke up. But I've forgotten it again though it was very important; I believe your face was a sign that something dreadful was coming true.'

'Oh dear,' mocked Nell.

'I still feel quite frightened,' said Laura. 'I wish I hadn't dreamed it; I wish we weren't going away today. It's given me a headache, too,' she added.

And when she got out of bed and looked at herself in the glass she found her face white with dark circles under the eyes.

'Lolly's got one of her headaches,' announced Nell later to explain her sister's lassitude during a bustled morning.

'What a day to choose for a headache,' said Birdie bitterly.

'A headache? Why didn't you come for one of my

capsules? You never take a remedy early enough,' complained her aunt.

But when they were finally off Laura's spirits rose; and by the time they were installed in a reserved compartment of the three o'clock train from Liverpool Street, with the foot-warmers on the carriage floor as hot as could be borne, and the assurance of a tea basket when they stopped at Ipswich, even Birdie forgot her anxieties and produced a book to read, while Mrs Young, very comfortable in her corner with cushions and a rug, thought that Nell might well let Shah out for a little bit. So Shah, whose childlike mew contrasted so sadly with his dignity, was released from his basket and nursed on Nell's lap and shown the country through which they were running, being held very firmly when the ticket collector came, and finally allowed a few drops of milk.

Laura had brought a book but she did not read. She stared instead at the flying landscape. A clear afternoon, brilliant between storms of hail, filled the countryside with a cold yellow light that turned the soaked fields into desolate spaces and made the cottages, pink-washed or white or blue, look snugger by comparison. Here a door swung open and she saw a fire burning; here some children in clumsy boots were carrying home a pail. It was the home-coming hour, Laura sadly told herself, but she and Nell were hurrying to a home not theirs. And she went on in her mind with a fanciful tale she had begun that morning while dressing. Suppose when she arrived at Yule Lodge she found it the house of her dream. What could she do? Could she refuse to live in it and take Nell away? The idea of living together in the prettiest house of their own, probably in the country and almost certainly by the sea, had for years been a favourite imagining of the sisters, and they had spent hours as children planning the details of the rooms. But, though Laura could picture herself defying her uncle: 'Nell is in danger here. She must not stay', though she could see herself driving back to the station with her sister, determined to set out for a safer home, her imagination refused to present a single practical detail. She had only once in her life bought herself a railway ticket and had never been allowed to travel alone.

The journey was nearly over. Birdie packed her book away and advised Nell to put Shah back in his basket. Mrs Young sat up and began to peer out of the window.

'The brougham is to be at the station,' she said. 'I wonder if we shall care for it. I believe it is very old fashioned; but we must make do with it till the new carriage is built.'

Their arrival made a stir. The station-master was waiting with Mr Young to greet them. Porters stared in open curiosity as they shouldered portmanteaux for the luggage cart; a man in livery collected the smaller things.

'This is Fred Thrower,' said Mr Young presenting him. 'He will be head coachman when his father retires.'

As the party appeared at the station door the elder Thrower, white and bent, climbed down from the box. His old monkey face had more sadness in it than pleasure and he shook his head mournfully when the ladies spoke to him, as if the change in his life had come too late and found him set in his ways, unable to be glad.

He showed agility however in disposing of the baggage and satisfied Mrs Young that, though old enough to be cautious, he was not too old to be a trustworthy driver. The pair of fat bays reassured her also; she murmured her approval as they left the station. She was less pleased with the carriage. It was, as she anticipated, very old fashioned: a double brougham, smelling of damp and not at all comfortable. Its only merit seemed its capacity; they all fitted in easily, Shah's basket and several other items included.

Laura where she sat could only just see out of the window, but when in the fading light they turned through a gate she felt that the curve of the drive was what she expected. The servants were waiting in the porch. Two pillars held up a semi-circular roof; at their base two globes like immense cannon balls kept carriage wheels from grazing the steps.

'Don't slip off,' warned Mr Young as Nell balanced herself on one of these to reach Shah's basket.

'They're Tweedledum and Tweedledee,' she cried, saying anything that came into her head in the excitement of arrival.

Mr Young laughed and Laura stopped short in the doorway. This was her nightmare; a joke and somebody laughing. She turned back abruptly and her uncle asked in alarm:

'Laura, what is the matter? Don't you feel well?'

'She has had a headache all day,' explained Mrs Young tranquilly, shaking out the folds of her cloak and going into the house without seeing her niece's face.

'I am sure you are all tired. Come up and take off your things. I will show you the bedrooms.'

Laura followed upstairs in a dream; carrying a wrap thrust upon her by someone else. She came at the end of the procession into her aunt's bedroom, dimly admired its splendours and turned to follow elsewhere. As they walked down the gallery Mr Young began to look mysterious and Nell cried suddenly:

'Are we coming to your surprise?'

'You are.'

He ushered them into a charming suite: bedrooms with a slip of a sitting room adjoining. The bedroom doors faced one another across a wide corridor; the sitting-room door was at right angles between. All three rooms could be shut off from the gallery by closing double doors in the connecting archway. One bedroom, furnished blue, faced the garden; the other room with decorations in pink overlooked the drive.

They were larger and more elegant than the girls expected, each with two windows reaching almost to the floor. But in the midst of the unfamiliarity Laura was overwhelmed by a sense of something familiar. This had all happened before; she had been in this very room. Perhaps longer ago than in her dreams, perhaps more than once. But the window opposite her door was the nightmare window; and as she looked at it a real fear, not the fear that comes in dreams, cut her off from the others into an appalling loneliness.

'I kept the old fourposters,' Mr Young was saying. 'Miss

Bird wanted me to get new French beds without canopies. But I have always known fourposters in these rooms and I did not like to change.'

'As if we minded – ' Nell was wild with delight. Her chatter completely covered Laura's silence. She danced round her uncle, pulled him into the other room and then darted back for Laura's candles so that the beauties of the blue patterned chintz might be more fully lighted. Birdie joined in with her shriller notes of admiration; then Mrs Young called and they all moved away. Their voices sounded from other parts of the house; Laura sat on in the twilight wondering what to do. A shadow crossed the window and she started and looked up. It was nothing; a bird had flown by. Her room looked straight into a knot of trees on the other side of the drive; she could see the last of the sunset through the criss-cross of bare branches, and from higher up in the treetops came a piercing chatter. Starlings in hundreds disturbed by the carriage, were settling again for the night.

'Quite a concert,' said Birdie, looking in and going out again when she saw only Laura there.

'I like the birds. They will be a help,' Laura whispered.

Presently she forced herself to go to the window. Nell came back and found her staring out. A small stone balcony outside was joined to a similar balcony at the window of the next room by a wide stone ledge. Ledge alternating with balcony ran the whole length of the front of the house.

'Is this the room you dreamed about?' asked Nell.

Laura nodded. 'I think so, though in my dreams it had one window, not two.'

Nell seemed at a loss and Laura felt ashamed of spoiling her pleasure in the new house. She determined to say one thing more and have done with the subject.

'Could you climb along here?' she asked and Nell looked out.

'Not easily, but I am sure I could.'

'Nell, will you promise me never to try? Please promise now, before you are a minute older.'

But Nell was excited and tired, and her sister's solemnity annoyed her.

'I won't promise. Lolly, you're being absurd. Nobody would try to walk along that ledge for fun, but if the house were on fire or Shah was in difficulties, I should certainly try. I'm sorry about your dream and I'm sorry it came this morning, but it was only a dream. You are not to fuss over me because you've had a nightmare. You've often had bad dreams before and you probably will again.'

Perhaps she felt she had been unkind, for late that night she crept into her sister's room.

'Lolly, are you asleep?'

Laura was not asleep. She had blown her candle out and was lying stiffly in bed, her face turned away from the window.

'Lolly, I'm so cold. Can I get in with you?'

'All right.' Laura's tone was grudging but Nell knew she was grateful. It was not for the elder sister to betray fear to the younger.

Nell got into the other half of the big bed. Her feet were icy and she moved them softly up and down the line of warmth that radiated from Laura. Presently she said:

'Are you still frightened of that window?'

'Not so much from here. In the dream I was standing by the door.'

'Lolly, shall we change rooms?'

Laura considered. 'No, Nell, I've thought of that. I don't think we can after Uncle has planned everything for us. It would look so ungrateful.'

'I'm afraid it would.'

There was a silence. Then Laura said:

'The rooms are so nice, really.'

'Wonderful. D'you know, Uncle has even made Birdie fasten chintz over the backs of our looking glasses because he thinks a dressing table should not be ugly at the back. I think there is something almost frightening about Uncle's surprises. We can't deserve so much.'

CHAPTER III

A SOUND night's rest did not dim Laura's recollection of the dream, but it gave her courage to face her fears. As she dressed the next morning she determined to be sensible. A strange thing had occurred, there was no denying that; she had been badly frightened and could by too much thinking frighten herself again. Whether her dream was a warning or a coincidence she could not tell, but she decided to say nothing more about it for the present. She would watch for danger by herself and if anything more occurred to alarm her she would speak to her uncle. Perhaps in any case she would tell him the story later on, when they were properly settled in their new home. Or better still, she perhaps might find an adviser, some old wise person, a friend of the family but not a relation, a doctor for instance, or a clergyman. She decided that a doctor might be unsympathetic; a clergyman ought to be interested in the gift of prophecy.

Amused with the conclusion of her thoughts she ran downstairs to breakfast. Mrs Young was staying in bed after the journey and so Laura sat behind the tray.

Birdie had breakfasted with them in schoolroom days, but now she insisted on an earlier meal for herself. She usually came to lunch unless the table was likely to be crowded, to dinner only on birthdays and on Christmas Day. When there was a tea party she poured out in the drawing room; care of many guests fatigued Mrs Young and Laura was too absent-minded to be trustworthy.

The morning was fine; Nell and her uncle chatted together in the highest of spirits. Laura looked curiously at him now and then, noticing a change in him that she could not at once define. She began by thinking that his clothes had changed him: he was punctilious in dress and she had never before seen him in a country coat and riding breeches. But the difference was more subtle than this: he seemed less on his guard, more carefree, a man at ease in his own place. She wondered if his attitude as guardian would alter; they would soon feel if this were so, being much more in his company now than before. She determined to discuss the matter with Nell.

'Since Lolly feels quite well again,' said Mr Young, 'suppose we do as I had planned and make a tour this morning. I should like to take you round the park and to the home farm. Will you be ready at eleven o'clock? Be well shod, mind; it is muddy underfoot.'

They joyfully agreed to meet him. Then Nell went upstairs to unpack her music and Laura decided to explore the lower part of the house again before her aunt came down. She peeped into her uncle's study and saw book-shelves and a gun rack, and into the morning room bright with chintzes where a good fire was burning and her aunt's embroidery and spectacle case were already set out. The door of the drawing room was muffled by a portière; Laura shut herself inside the quiet room.

It was very large, light and a little cold-looking. The colours were not what she had learned to admire – she missed the soft tones of the Norwood house – but they were uncommon enough to arouse her interest, and though Mrs Young the evening before had said 'ugly' as she looked round in lamplight, Laura could not agree.

The wallpaper was grey, a delicate pattern of vine leaves in faint grey upon a fainter ground. Shadows on them were touched with thin lines of crimson, and a strip of paper painted to look like crimson braid outlined the doors and the four edges of each wall. Tasselled bell-ropes of crimson cord hung by the mantelpiece; above it rose a stately looking-glass with brackets fastened to the wall at equal intervals round it.

Crimson plush covered the brackets, each of which held a thin cup and saucer of Chinese grey. On the white marble mantelpiece stood white vases with crystal lustres, their coldness reflected in the glass behind them; and in the long mirror of a consol table against another wall waxed fruits in a case gleamed a soft white. In contrast to these quiet tones the doors, window frames and wainscoting had been varnished golden yellow; and into the wall on either side of the bay window was let a slab of yellow marble, tall and vivid in colour, reaching from floor to ceiling, quite unlike anything Laura had ever known.

Someone, she thought, had planned with care this crimson, grey and gold. The cushions, now faded, had once been of yellow silk; the glazed chintz on the sofa showed a pattern of plum colour on grey. Some of the occasional chairs were gilded like the mirrors, and the bosses of the mantelpiece had yellow marble inlet. She tried to picture the woman for whom these colours had been chosen. Was it someone as dark as herself or as fair as Nell?

A clock struck and she started. When Laura was mooning, as her sister called it, she lost all sense of time. But she and Nell were ready long before eleven; they went into the morning room to wait. Mrs Young was not yet down, so Laura opened the door into the conservatory and wandered about admiring the ferns.

Suddenly a gardener came in with a watering can. He was a fat man with a good-natured brown face and he beamed at Laura in great friendliness as she said good-day.

'What pretty baskets of ferns they are,' she added politely, feeling that the encounter demanded some graciousness from herself.

Delighted with the opening, the gardener began to talk about the plants, and walked her up and down explaining how he treated them in such a broad Norfolk accent that she could not understand him. She did her best to play a part, smiling and admiring zealously, conscious that her shyness was making her overact, conscious too of Nell in the morning room behind her, overhearing everything but keeping herself safe.

At last Nell called quietly, 'Here's Uncle to the rescue,' and in a minute Mr Young came out to take his niece away. He was amused at her predicament.

'You must learn to talk Norfolk, my dears,' he laughed as they walked off.

'I've learned my first sentence,' boasted Nell. 'Listen.' She tucked her chin absurdly into her neck and croaked a few words in an unnatural guttural.

'Who taught you that?' asked Laura.

' "Will you want any more hot water?" That's how the housemaid asked me when she brought my bath. Didn't you notice, Lolly?'

'Now, Nell, if you will stop your chatter I will show you what is to my mind the most serious defect of the house.' Mr Young stood still in the drive and pointed with his cane. 'Do you see that the front with its balconies and tall windows and balustrade running along the roof is all really false? If you go back to the drawing-room windows you will see a very different style. The original front was masked by my grandfather in a sudden fit of extravagance. His money ran short before he had time to make further alterations, and if I were a rich man I should pull down all this grandeur and restore the original simplicity. A sketch of the house as it used to be hangs in my study.'

Laura glanced a little fearfully at her bedroom window. She saw what her uncle meant: the mouldings, the squat balconies, even the ledge connecting them, were clumsy additions, standing out in relief too bold from the surface they were meant to adorn. She wondered for a moment if the history of her family might contain some explanation of her dream. But as she wondered she dismissed the thought; her dream touched the future, not the past. Of this she was confident, though she could not tell why.

Gardens, greenhouses and stables were visited in order. Everything they saw delighted the girls and their abundant satisfaction pleased their guide. A warmth, almost a tenderness, thawed Mr Young's reserve; his nieces were closer in sympathy with him than they had ever been. He took pride in introducing them to the men on the estate; 'Mr Ralph's children,' he said to the older hands. One of the gardeners looked at the girls admiringly; 'Them'll marry and go away too soon,' he declared. Mr Young was still chuckling over the remark when they left the garden and set out for the home farm. Here were more introductions, more things to be seen. Beyond the farm a track ran through a pasture, and beyond that again the ground fell away, sloping gently to the village and then to the river. They walked to a stile in a near hedge and looked over it.

'That smoke comes from my cottages in the village,' said Mr Young 'and the house in the trees belongs to one of my tenants, a Mr Fraser whom you will see on Sunday in church. There's the church, and the parsonage to the right of it. The river runs on the far side of those meadows; you'll go boating on it later in the year.'

They turned to make their way home by a new path. The elms that fringed the field were a deep copper red at the top, but the oaks dotting the park looked wintry still. Through the grey green of their branches shone the white house, lighted now by a gleam of clear March sun.

'How friendly it looks from here,' exclaimed Laura. 'I am so glad I have seen this view of it.'

'I like this aspect best,' agreed her uncle. 'When I was a boy it was this side I pictured most often to myself.'

'Were you away from home, then, when you were a boy?'

'Yes; I think, in fact, I am fonder of this place because I was banished so often from it during much of my childhood.'

'Banished?'

'It is a curious tale. Our mother died when I was eight and your father was six. She had been ailing for a long time and we had been allowed to run wild. Ralph was a pet of the grooms and spent most of his time in the stables, but I was shy and afraid of horses. I remember being much by myself.

We both kept out of our father's way; he hated children, and the very sight of our dirty hands and unbrushed hair made him angry. We used to hide if we heard him coming.

'Well, he was left with two undisciplined boys on his hands and he made short work of the problem. He put us under a tutor. Somebody recommended a Mr White on the other side of the county, a clergyman who took pupils to bring up with his own sons. I don't imagine my father made a single enquiry, but luckily for us the Whites were excellent people. We must have been a great trouble to them, we could neither read nor write. Mrs White taught us at first, then her husband took us on.'

'Did you like the other children?'

'I believe so, but I liked the parents more. I respected White deeply; I owe many of my principles to his teaching. My father, if he had known, would never have sent us to him. White talked what was known as Christian Socialism; indeed, he preached his views and got into serious trouble in consequence. Finally he turned Unitarian and left the Church.'

'Was it a nice vicarage?'

'No, a mean little place; I was often homesick for more liberty. The Whites knew this; they were kind people and encouraged me to talk about my home. He used to remind me of my responsibilities as heir and tell me how much good I could do as a landowner. My father would have thought him mad.'

'Did you ever go home?'

'Three times in five years. It seems curious to me now that we didn't forget the place, but we never wavered in the certainty that we were only staying at the vicarage and that Yule was our real home. Then my father married again.'

Mr Young paused to flick a twig from the grass into the bushes.

'You will find a small portrait of my stepmother in the morning room. It is very like but it doesn't do her justice. She was extraordinarily captivating. We boys were too young to appreciate her charm but we felt the warmth and liveliness she carried with her; she seemed to change the whole house. She persuaded my father to send us to school – indeed our manners had grown rustic – and to let us come to Yule for the holidays. He was surly enough when we came. I think he was jealous, perhaps, for we were nearer her age than he.'

'Was she dark or fair?'

'Fair, with dark eyes; a remarkable colouring. Mrs Fraser, whose house I showed you in the village, is a little like her, but without the same vivacity.'

'Go on, uncle,' urged Nell.

'Well, they lived in great happiness for over two years and then she died suddenly. She neglected a cold and then caught a fever visiting one of the cottages. I think the old doctor mismanaged the case: nobody had believed there was any cause for alarm. We were away at school and of course knew very little, but afterwards I heard all sorts of stories: that my father had forced her to go out while she was still weak, that she had gone walking in the wet against his wishes. It was clear that there had been some neglect or mistaken treatment and my father never got over her loss. He would not let us come home, shut up half the house, refused visitors and lived by himself, seldom going outside the bounds of his own property. He began to have a horror of strangers; he was kind enough to his servants and to tenants already on the estate, but would not allow a new servant into the house and I am told he let cottages stand empty for years rather than admit labourers whom he did not know. When we grew up he made no difference in his attitude towards us. He seemed determined that we should not come home and he used influence to get us both settled in India, your father as a soldier and me as a civilian.'

'Why did you go? Couldn't you have refused?'

'We could have refused, I suppose,' said Mr Young. 'Indeed, for me it was a great mistake to accept the offer. But I felt that if I could not be at home I might as well be at the other end of the earth. So out I went dutifully, and so did your father; we both married in India and you know the rest of the story.'

'Not entirely, Uncle; what made you come home?'

'Ill health, my dear, I could not stand the climate. When you two were left orphans so suddenly I was ill myself and could not help. That was why my friends brought you home and settled you with your grandmother. I had to retire long before my time was up.'

'And then?'

'Why, then the same old difficulty. I hankered for Norfolk and could not fancy settling elsewhere. So after a year or two, when I was fit again, I went to visit my father. I came to stay in the neighbourhood and heard many stories about him: that he was ill and would not see a doctor, that he never went to church because he thought the parson was in league with the devil, that he hated new clothes and went about in rags like a scarecrow, that his old servants were idle and that his tenants robbed him. At last I determined to see for myself. I drove over one afternoon and as soon as I turned in at the gate I saw the old man hobbling out in a great rage to meet me. He knew me a long way off – he had an eye like a hawk's – and directly I drew up he shouted, "You're Walter, come after your property. Well, you're too early; I'm not dead yet." You would hardly have understood him, Laura, he talked so broad. Old people do, you know, if they live alone with servants. I was quite shocked to see him, he looked so old and ill. But he still had force enough to refuse me admittance, so I jumped down and said as coolly as I could:

"I've come to ask questions about the property. If I'm to inherit it, won't you tell me how you would like it kept?"

'That surprised him; I could see he was not displeased. "Well, come in," he grumbled and he took me in to dinner. The house was dirty and shabby; I don't suppose so much as a mat had been renewed in twenty years. The old housekeeper burst into tears when I went to visit her. She had kept the place in order as long as she could, but the work was beyond her; and the master, she said, was going very queer. I stayed all afternoon walking and talking with my father. I said I would like to come again and I told him I was married. Then I saw for the first time that he was more than eccentric. He gave me an odd look, I cannot describe it. But he said nothing till I was leaving and then he jerked out, "You come back again. But I won't have your missus here. Is that plain?"

'And so I got into the habit, as you know, of coming down here to stay with him and I gradually took over the management of the property. I had to leave your aunt behind when I made these visits, but when you girls came to live with us she was not so much alone.'

'Did Grandfather grow fond of you?'

Mr Young reflected. 'No, as far as I can judge we were never fond of each other; but I think in the end I won his respect. Before he died he knew that I loved the place and that my object was to do the best I could for it. But it was many years before he let me have the least authority. His jealousy at first was a sort of madness too.'

'And now that it is yours, Uncle, will you make many changes?'

'No, Nell, I must confess I have few grand schemes. I shall make one or two alterations in the garden – cut back the shrubberies, for instance, to leave room for a lawn tennis court. I shall build some new cottages and improve the existing ones; I want my tenants to be contented and happy. And I should like my family to be happy too. Your aunt, I think, will benefit from the air; she was surprised this morning to find how well she had slept. And you will meet some delightful young people; there are several families in the neighbourhood waiting to call. I should like my niece-daughters, with their pleasant looks, to crown my work by making my home pleasant, so that people may come to it eagerly and my friends envy me, and that you yourselves when you marry may look back with satisfaction to your days in this house.'

The emotion in his voice affected his nieces; they went indoors with grave faces. As Laura was washing her hands before lunch Nell came into her room and said thoughtfully, 'I do wish Uncle and Aunt had a son.'

'Not an only son, for if anything happened to him how terrible it would be.'

'A great many sons, then. Of course with a large family everything might be different. If you have a great many children I am sure you can't mind so much about each one.'

Birdie caught the last remark as she joined the girls on their way downstairs. 'You would not speak like that, Nell, if you were one of a number. There were fifteen of us, and my dear mother used to boast that she loved all alike. I remember her telling us often that the capacity to love each child as it comes is one of the miracles of motherhood.'

CHAPTER IV

MRS YOUNG made enquiries about the church in Yule and found that arrangements were exactly as she liked. Ante-Communion service on the first and third Sundays, Morning Prayer with the litany on the Sundays between. Some people prefer shorter services at irregular hours; she did not object to length at a convenient time. Her husband might sigh as he shifted his position, stiffness in the back was for her part of the rite. She followed psalms, prayers, lessons, with minute observance from an enormous book and sat through the sermon without stirring unless the preacher was unusually long-winded. Then she would sometimes glance sideways as her husband took out his watch, and frowned if the big hand was near the half hour. She disliked having to hurry back for lunch.

The present rector of Yule had held the living for six years but he was still known in the village as the new parson. This was partly because his ways were strange to his congregation. He was an earnest young man who intoned responses and put his choir into surplices. He had also effected changes in the seating of the church; the old pews were replaced by yellow benches that smelt strongly of varnish. The front bench was reserved for the Lodge; and when the family made their first appearance in church they found that Birdie had come in ahead of them and taken up a position at one end of the row. Nell and Mrs Young filed in successively, but Laura, afraid of crowding her aunt, passed round the front of the bench and settled herself in a chair under the pulpit. She nodded briefly in response to Birdie's signals; it was of no consequence to her where she sat. But Birdie was overcome to find herself in Laura's place and forced to keep it since her way out was blocked by a pillar. She nodded and pointed and raised many unhappy eyebrows, only stopping at last when Laura scowled. Nell, fixed in between Birdie and Aunt Carrie, looked on with glee at the pantomime and stared cruelly at her sister all through it. Laura was careful to avoid these glances; the determined gleam in Nell's eyes too often made her laugh.

Though shy to find herself at right angles to the congregation and so exposed to its curious gaze, Laura realized as soon as the service began that her post had its advantages. When the eyes of the others were drawn to the chancel she could look about her without seeming to stare.

Past the decent rank of her well-dressed family she could see the front pews on the other side of the aisle. Here sat the Rector's wife with her four stolid children, and behind them the Miss Veaseys, who were the first to call at the Lodge. When she next looked up Laura's eyes travelled further and suddenly they were met by a twinkling gleam. She turned away, then peeped again; an old man was looking at her, a man with white hair and a neat white beard. He had evidently noticed her lack of attention and the amusement in his face was a comment on the fact. Laura disregarded him by looking sternly past him and suddenly her heart gave a throb of delight. Beside the man sat three small children, and beyond them, under the wall, a young woman of quite remarkable beauty. Laura, dark herself, loved fair hair, and she could not help staring at this remarkable stranger, speculating about her and presently in a sort of rapture designing her portrait. The clear window above the young woman showed a sky alternately white and blue, and the sun, glancing in from somewhere in the chancel that Laura could not see, blazed and dulled by turns, throwing golden lights from time to time on the sitter's quiet face.

Painting in imagination, Laura sat wrapt through the sermon and rose for the last hymn determined to discover this family's name. There had been greetings and introductions as the Youngs came to church, there would surely be more still as they went away.

But during the hymn a small commotion arose in the distant pew. The young woman, clearly the mother, bent down to a little girl. Something was the matter, the child was crying. Signals passed between members of the family, then the two slipped out and went away together, the boys staying unconcerned beside the man. And in the churchyard there was such a muddle of presentations, so many people crowding to speak, that though Laura saw her uncle talking to the stranger and though he looked at her again with a twinkling smile, he was not introduced to her or to Nell and they started home again without learning his name.

'Uncle,' demanded Laura when they were halfway up the hill, 'who was the man with the two little boys? I saw you talking to him after the service. He has such a lively face.'

'That is George Fraser, my tenant at The Shrubbery. He is an interesting fellow; we call him the poet.'

'Is he a poet?'

'Well, he made his name as a young man by writing poetry. I wonder you have none of you heard of him. He has also done a good deal of translation from the German, and now that he is married again and has a young family he has begun to write novels. I don't care for them so much myself, but I believe they have a great vogue in ladies' circulating libraries.'

'George Fraser,' mused Laura. 'Why, Aunt Carrie, we have read one of his books. Don't you remember *The Career of Ronald Carfax*? We had it from the library only last autumn.'

Mrs Young was uncertain. 'You know,' persisted Laura. 'There was a count in it who killed a dog with a poisoned rapier.'

'Oh, yes. But were there not some very sordid chapters: common people speaking a dialect I could not understand?'

'There is dialect in Fraser's work,' commented Mr

Young. 'He draws on his experiences as a student in Edinburgh.'

'Then that was his wife in church with him,' exclaimed Laura suddenly.

'Yes, there is a considerable difference in age. Indeed, by a first wife he has a daughter not much younger.'

'Did we see her?' enquired Mrs Young.

'No, she is in London. And Fraser asked me to apologize. He and his wife are going up to visit her and will not be able to call on us during the next fortnight. I gather that they are concerned about the daughter; she has been overworking at college and is ill.'

'College?' cried Laura and Nell simultaneously.

'She is a learned young lady,' their uncle warned them.

'Oh dear,' sighed Nell, 'shall we like her, Uncle?'

'I must confess I find her somewhat alarming.'

Laura's face fell but Nell cried unafraid, 'He is only saying that to tease us, Lolly. I gave up believing in Uncle after he told us poor little Lucy Long was strong-minded.'

'I protest,' said Mr Young. 'I said nothing so unkind.'

'Oh yes, indeed. Didn't he, Lolly?'

'And the young lady never deserved the epithet?'

'Oh well, we admit we knew what you meant.'

They always did know what Mr Young meant. He took a curious pleasure in scrutinizing their friends and the girls were sometimes disconcerted by the quickness of his intuitions. His comments could be painfully shrewd.

In this case his description was certainly just. Laura, summoned to the drawing room about three weeks later when Mrs Fraser came with her step-daughter to call, found in the latter a sedateness and assurance that alarmed her and would, she knew, unfailingly irritate her uncle. He liked girls to be uncertain, even shy. Miss Fraser was not bold, but her manner was calm and when spoken to she paused as if to weigh question and answer before committing herself in reply. She was plainly, almost sternly dressed. Laura felt disappointed. The pale cheeks and tired eyes were the result of illness, but even allowing for this she found that Miss Fraser's stolid face lacked the humour and mobility of her father's expression. Could a poet's daughter, she wondered, possibly be dull?

She looked at the wife and again felt a surging of keen pleasure before the quiet radiance of her beauty. Mrs Fraser seemed to rest in an assurance of happiness; tranquillity made part of her charm. Nell for all her prettiness looked immature by contrast; her bright face had too little to tell.

But conversation languished; the ladies were difficult. The daughter seemed too serious, the stepmother shy. Mrs Young was never quick in giving openings and the quarter of an hour was passing heavily when Mrs Fraser, glancing at the tasselled velvet that covered the mantelpiece, remarked, 'I am glad you have not made many changes in this room.'

'You know the house?' Mrs Young spoke without thinking.

'Oh yes. I used to come, you know, and read to the old squire.'

Nell saw such blank amazement spread in her aunt's face that she sprang into the conversation.

'Did you really come here? I thought my grandfather was a sort of ogre.'

'He was, in a way, but a very lonely one,' Mrs Fraser explained. 'Of course, the people round here tell such absurd stories about him and we were warned when we came to The Shrubbery that he did not care for strangers. But he met my husband one day and took a fancy to him and sometimes used to ask him to the Lodge. And one day he passed in his pony carriage when I was out with the children. He stared so that I felt quite unhappy; for he looked old, you know, and lonely, and I knew he disliked meeting young people and children. But after that he sometimes mentioned me to my husband and one day when he was complaining that time went so slowly, Mr Fraser asked if he would like me to come and read to him. That was how it began.'

'My husband never told me,' said Mrs Young, still a little incredulous.

'Perhaps he did not realize how often I came. I didn't like to disturb him; he was always so busy. I used to come in by the garden door and the housekeeper took me upstairs. The old man was usually in bed, sometimes in a chair. If I read long enough I could send him to sleep.'

'What did you read?' Nell asked; her aunt seemed more at a loss with each revelation.

'The psalms from the prayer book,' replied Mrs Fraser. 'I read them over and over again. He liked joining in if he knew the verses. The day before he died he was very feeble, but I could just hear a murmur as I read psalm ninety. You know, "The days of our age are threescore years and ten." It was so pathetic; I could hardly go on.' Tears stood in her eyes.

Laura turned to her glowing. 'Oh,' she exclaimed, 'I am sure you read aloud very beautifully.'

Mrs Fraser made no disclaimer. 'My husband taught me. I often read to him,' she said.

Then she stood up to go. Mrs Young rose with determination and motioned Laura to pull the bell. Both nieces knew, as she wished her callers goodbye, that she had been shocked into strong disapproval by the afternoon's disclosures. And though her husband laughed at her when she met him with her complaints, and she admitted under pressure that the poet looked agreeable and that his daughter seemed a sensible, quiet girl, no amount of teasing could shake her attitude towards Mrs Fraser. At a mere mention of the name she would purse her lips.

She cherished her disapproval, and the families did not meet. Laura and Nell complained to one another that their nearest neighbours and the most interesting people they had so far encountered – though on this point Laura was more emphatic than Nell – were also the people they most seldom saw. The house was deserted when Mrs Young returned their call; after knocking and ringing vainly several times the man left their cards in the porch. And an invitation to tea, sent tardily from The Shrubbery a few weeks later, named a day when aunt and neices were unhappily pledged elsewhere. Nor were the Frasers to be met at other houses. They did not keep a carriage and stayed very much at home. But everyone was willing to talk about them; the conversation quickened whenever their name was mentioned and the rigid joined in with the frivolous in picking over gossip. Most people liked the poet; his neighbourhood was evidently proud of him. But his wife and daughter were called difficult and unsociable and the younger children were dismissed as very badly brought up.

This general disapproval amused the girls, but it brought them no nearer to an acquaintance with the Frasers, and the Sunday encounters meanwhile dwindled to mere bows and smiles. At last one evening in April Laura met them again. She had gone out to sketch in a paddock shut off by woods from the house. A right of way crossed it, with a stile at each end, and Laura settled herself in the middle of the field. She wanted to draw tree tops against an evening sky; the lines of branches softened now by a powdering of green would in all too short a time be lost in leaves. This coming of spring in the country enraptured her; she seized every moment she could get to paint or to draw. Tonight she had not wasted time in a search for a camp stool but had come rushing out with a shooting-stick snatched from the hall. It was uncomfortable to sit on, but she soon forgot about it, enjoying as she worked the evening quiet around her.

Presently a figure moved in the woods and George Fraser climbed the stile and came slowly towards her. His chin was sunk, his hands clasped behind him; he was so deep in thought that he did not notice her. Laura hated being discovered at work, but planted as she was in the middle of a field she could not very well go away without seeming rude. So she sat where she was, pretending to draw and glad that her page had so little to show. The poet came on steadily; she began to feel foolish. She cleared her throat, but he did not hear her. At last, when he was quite close, she clapped her book. He came to himself with a violent start.

'Miss Young! Was I asleep? Have you been here all the time or have you sprung out of the ground by magic?'

He seemed so startled that Laura apologized. 'I am so sorry I made you jump. I could have called out before you came so close, but I didn't like to disturb you.'

Her penitent tones amused him, and instead of walking on he stopped to see what she had drawn. Laura tried to hide it from him without seeming to do so, lost her balance on the stick and shot at his feet half a dozen loose pages from her sketch-book, the picture she least wished to show falling out face uppermost. This, done in a moment of great ardour some months before, was a tinted sketch showing three damsels of extreme attenuation bringing food and wine to a fainting youth with long curled hair. Mr Fraser did not pretend to ignore it.

'I prefer robuster types myself,' he said as he passed it back. 'But my daughter is entirely of your opinion. Burne-Jones, I understand, is the god of her art school.'

An eagerness broke through Laura's deep confusion. 'Oh, does Miss Fraser go to an art school in London?'

'She does. But she can speak for herself.' And Laura turned to find that the girl with her two little brothers had followed him up the path. All three carried baskets of primroses. 'Come here and be introduced,' the poet called to his sons. 'This is James and this is Robert,' he explained to Laura, while the boys put down their baskets and offered her very dirty hands. Then they fell back a short distance, staring with the cautiousness of little animals, while Margaret Fraser came close and looked longingly at the sketch-book.

'I didn't know you liked drawing,' she said. 'Please may I look?'

'Oh no,' answered Laura hastily. 'It's only rubbish. I put all sorts of nonsense into this book.' Then the disappointment in the other's face made her feel ashamed of her rudeness and she added, 'If I show you my pictures, will you let me see yours?'

'Of course I will.' When Margaret Fraser felt interest her whole face changed. The stolid features lifted and became expressive, their alertness demanded a response. 'She is really quite handsome,' thought Laura in surprise, and the two stared at each other for the first time with friendliness, each assessing what she found in the other's face.

'Do you paint landscape?' ventured Laura. 'Couldn't we go out together sometimes? I am sure you must know all the pretty places round here.'

The pleasure deepened in Margaret's look, but before she found words her father answered. 'Done,' he cried with enthusiasm. 'Miss Young, you have asked the very question I had hoped for. Poor Margaret is to stay the whole of this term away from College; the doctor will not let her go back yet. She was complaining only today that there was no one in the village whose tastes ran with hers, and by a piece of luck here we find you sketching. If you will come to The Shrubbery and arrange an expedition I promise that you may later draw aesthetic portraits of me and all my family – and you can make these dirty boys look as fragile as you please.'

His hearty acceptance left no room for Margaret's answer and she looked slightly put out. Under cover of his vehemence however the girls exchanged glances, coming almost unconsciously to an understanding. Laura knew as they walked away that she would meet them again very soon.

CHAPTER V

NELL in many ways acted as her sister's guardian, and one of her tasks was the lopping of enthusiasms. Lolly's sudden crazes and violent admirations would shoot into monstrous growths in the course of a few days if Nell's comments, sometimes cutting indeed, did not act as a pruning hook. Nell had teased her sister out of many extravagances and Laura seldom bore her any ill will. If she was hot for a cause she could laugh at herself. If she admired a person too much she sometimes quarrelled with Nell.

And now, as Nell complained, Lolly talked of nothing but the Frasers; not of an individual moreover but of the entire family. First, there was the poet; well, Nell admired him too. She was quite willing to join her sister there. Then Mrs Fraser. Nell admitted she was beautiful; 'but I don't see, Lolly, why you make quite such a fuss.' And finally Margaret. Here the younger girl was scornful. 'I don't think she's in the least interesting. She's simply a dull person who has been to college, and the only thing she has ever done is to read a lot of books.'

'Well, I should like to read a lot of books too.'

And Nell retorted, maddeningly, 'They'd do you no good.'

But for all her scorn Nell was inquisitive; and when the days passed without bringing any word from The Shrubbery she was the first to comment upon the fact and to wonder why Margaret made no sign.

'What did she say, Lolly, shen she asked you to go sketching?'

'Nothing definite. We made no plans.'

'I expect the arrangement was that you should write.'

Laura denied this and the next day Nell added, 'Well, why don't you write all the same?'

'Shall I?' Laura had already thought of doing so and Nell's encouragement sent her now to the escritoire in the morning room, where she chose some fine notepaper and a broad pen, and then wrote 'Dear Miss Fraser' in her boldest hand.

There followed a long pause. She wanted an opening, something remarkable yet not at all silly. No inspiration came to her from the peaceful room; Aunt Carrie clicked her crochet hook and and the clock struck two. The bright sunshine outside provided a topic; she dipped her pen in the ink once more and began "The weather". Almost immediately came an interruption: Mrs Young wanted the blind drawn down. The telling sentence slipped from Laura's mind as she rose, and when she sat down again "The weather" looked so banal, such a commonplace opening for a witty note, that she tore up the sheet and started afresh. Nell came back, dressed for the carriage, to find her folding up the letter.

'Still here, Laura? You must have written pages.'

'Only half a sheet,' mumbled her sister.

'Do let me see what you have said.'

'Of course not,' returned Laura with dignity, licking up the envelope as quickly as possible.

'Volumes torn up,' continued the gadfly, lifting the wastepaper-basket and peering in.

'Go away,' begged Laura and Mrs Young remarked, 'Nell, my dear, have you nothing to do?' At this rebuke Nell subsided into silence and Laura was able to write the address in peace.

There was no hiding the reply when it came. She was struggling with the accompaniment of one of Nell's new songs when a note was brought to her in the drawing room with the information that the Master Frasers were waiting for an answer but would not come in.

'Let me see.' Nell peered over her sister's shoulder. 'What

a learned looking writing – so small, just like a man's. And what queer *e*'s.'

Margaret Fraser affected a Greek *e* and a fine clear script that was perhaps a shade too careful. Laura felt this without thinking about it. She was afire to answer the note.

'She has had a cold in her eyes, that's why she hasn't written. She wants me to suggest a day next week. Where's Aunt Carrie? I must ask what we are doing.'

The next week proved disappointingly full. Mrs Young was sure they had not an afternoon to spare. Laura in her answer could only suggest a morning expedition, with the possibility of a longer time at a later date. She took the note to the little boys, with an offer of milk and cake, but the two boys stared gravely at the sisters and refused.

'We were told not to go in because we are dusty,' explained the elder. And without more words they turned and ran off.

The appointed morning brought perplexities for Laura. The weather was treacherous, a brilliant sun alternating with showers.

'A pretty light for painting,' she ventured at breakfast.

'My dear, they will never expect you today,' exclaimed her aunt.

By eleven o'clock she had passed so often from hope to despair that she could bear the indecision no longer. No message had come to put her off, and so in a fine interval she slipped out of the house determined to discover whether her new friend was expecting her and what she meant to do. She was sure she could get quickly to The Shrubbery and back if she went by the right of way across the fields, and she set out recklessly in spite of the weather. It was a fortnight since she had sketched here and the spring had burst out since in fountains of green. The right of way was now a wrinkled line across a grassy sea. Mud oozed between the short blades under her feet, deluges of water slipped from long grass on either side. She lifted her skirts and the wet stalks whipped her ankles; a cascade fell from the bushes as she climbed the stile.

But a sort of intoxication carried her onwards, never had she found green so brilliant, so soft. Then the sky darkened, the vivid colour threatened, and another storm burst as she reached the Frasers' gate. She hopped across the mud to the shelter of their trees and hurried down the drive with as much dignity as her draggled condition would allow. The front door stood open and as the rain was beating into the porch she stepped just inside the hall and stood waiting for someone to answer her bell.

'Hullo,' called a child's voice. Robert Fraser was lying on his stomach in the alcove under the stairs. He was painting, and as she came up he washed out his brush noisily in a cup of very dirty water.

'I was sent out here,' he explained, 'because they thought I was going to be tiresome."

Laura looked puzzled.

'Mother's reading,' he said. 'They're all in the schoolroom listening.'

'Oh,' she cried, 'is your mother really reading aloud?'

He nodded. 'You can go in,' he told her, beginning to paint again.

All the doors round her were ajar but one. Before this one Laura stood hesitating while Robert eyed her quizzically. His stare embarrassed her, but she was too shy to make an entry. While she was waiting, however, someone turned the handle from inside. Margaret had heard voices and came out to see who it was. Her face lit up when she discovered Laura, but she shut the door behind her before speaking.

'I am so glad you are here,' she whispered, seizing Laura's arm. 'I couldn't send a message and I wondered what you would do. Will you come in and listen to the reading?'

The boy was gathering up his painting things. 'Margaret, let me in. I've changed my mind about making a noise.'

'Come along then, Robbie. But hurry up.'

Mr Fraser was so plainly impatient of interruption that when they came into the room Robert dived under the table, where James and his little sister were already settled with a paint-box between them and Margaret pulled Laura quickly down on the sofa beside her. Mrs Fraser smiled without leaving her place on the window seat, but her husband hardly seemed to see the girls. He was sunk in an old armchair with his legs on a stool. His feet stuck up defiantly in frayed carpet slippers. He was clearly in a very bad mood.

'Very well then,' said Mrs Fraser, as if in answer to a request already made, ' "James Lee" it shall be as soon as I can find the place.'

She put down one volume and opened another. While she was turning the pages Laura glanced about and found herself in a room very often described by other people when the Frasers came under discussion. 'One of the best rooms in that nice house,' the Miss Veaseys had moaned. 'So shabby and untidy,' the Rector's wife added. Shabby and untidy it certainly was: fishing rods, croquet mallets, bows and arrows cluttered up a corner; lesson books, a globe, a sewing machine and a Noah's ark stood closely packed on the top of a cupboard. The carpet was worn to threads, the bare table was slashed and ink-stained. Yet daffodils and green sprays filled the vases, and the curtains on either side the cheerful windows were of a curiously patterned stuff, blue on a white ground, that pleased Laura's eye.

Mrs Fraser found the place and began to read. 'Not much expression,' thought the girl at first, remembering Birdie's recitations. Then the quiet flow of the voice carried away her attention and she forgot the speaker, forgot her surroundings, forgot everything but the poem. But could she understand what the poem was about? The music sounded, the words escaped. Every now and then a phrase stood plain: here was someone unhappy, appealing to a man who did not love her. But no sooner did the drift of a passage become clear than the passage ended abruptly, like a section in a book, and a new part began, sometimes with a short title like a chapter heading.

' "By the drawing board," ' read Mrs Fraser, and Laura felt self-conscious. No one looked at her, however, they were all too much absorbed. When Mrs Fraser came to the end of the fragment she paused, stared thoughtfully at her husband and said, 'I don't quite follow that.'

'Do you see what it means?' asked Margaret of her friend.

Laura's only answer was a deep unhappy blush, and Mr Fraser, looking at her for the first time since she came into the room, observed tranquilly, 'She hasn't the least idea.'

'I'll finish,' said his wife, and read to the end.

Laura felt the poet's eye on her. 'Do you like it?' he enquired in the silence that followed. She reddened again and steadied herself enough to say, 'I think I should like it very much if I were used to it.'

'Well spoken, well spoken,' he cried, amused. 'Let us get used to it, then. There is just time to have the whole thing through again.'

'Oh, I am so sorry,' faltered Laura. 'I am afraid I must go or I shall be late for luncheon. It is not raining too hard now.'

'Nonsense,' exclaimed Mr Fraser impatiently. 'Stay where you are; you will get soaked.'

'My dear, you must stay to lunch with us,' said his wife. 'Our garden boy can go round to the Lodge and explain what has become of you.' And she sent Margaret off in search of the boy.

Margaret was gone some time. Mr Fraser drummed with his fingers on the arm of his chair, crossed and uncrossed his legs and said nothing. Every minute Laura expected him to get up in a fury and fling out of the room. The children under the table, quiet as mice, looked up with startled eyes whenever he moved, ready to scuttle at the first sign of alarm. Only the presence of his wife kept the room in order; and she perhaps was unconscious of this, for she stared out of the window dreaming, one hand holding her book, the other laid along the sill. Her tranquillity seemed a spell.

At last Margaret came back. 'Fred has gone to his dinner but Bessy says he will be here again in twenty minutes and she will send him as soon as he comes.'

'Twenty minutes from now will give time enough to let

them know,' said her stepmother, taking up the book again.

When she had finished the sun was shining. Laura looked up in surprise and Mr Fraser rose with a great bound and opened the French window.

> 'The swallow has set her six young on the rail
> And looks seaward,'

he shouted as he strode into the garden. His wife and daughter glanced at one another with a smile.

'Oh dear,' said Margaret, 'now he has something to boom. Now we shall hear nothing for days but that swallow. Father will come booming round corners and chant it at meals.'

'Still, even that is better – ' murmured Mrs Fraser.

'Oh yes,' Margaret turned to explain to Laura. 'My father has been thinking about Robert Browning lately and yesterday he looked again at his last book of verse. He didn't like it very much when he bought it and yesterday he was even more disappointed. He was dreadfully depressed last evening at supper and talked of the decay of a man's abilities after sixty till he made us feel quite unhappy too. So this morning we read some of the old poems to cheer ourselves up.'

'Was that Robert Browning you were reading?' Laura asked. 'Why, I thought nobody could understand what he wrote.'

Mrs and Miss Fraser burst out laughing. 'You mustn't say things like that here,' Margaret warned her. 'In this house we are all devotees. Why, my father wants to help found a society simply for studying the poems and teaching people to appreciate them. Perhaps I may go to the meetings when I am in London.'

'Do let me come again when you are reading,' begged Laura. Then she caught sight of the clock and sprang to her feet. There was still time to go back to her own house for lunch. 'I think I had better. Please forgive me for seeming rude. My aunt has plans for the afternoon and she will feel unsettled if I stay away.'

They did not try to keep her. 'James,' commanded his mother, 'get up and go to the gate with Miss Young.'

'Go along, James Lee,' said Robert from under the table.

James ran back and aimed a kick at his brother. Robbie caught his ankle, the cup of paint water went over in the scuffle, and Laura did not wait. She reflected as she hurried down the drive that the Fraser children were very badly brought up; even Margaret spoke too freely of her father. Then a wave of delight broke over her mind, carrying petty thoughts with it. What a morning she had spent! That was poetry. That was how poetry should be heard: read aloud and then gone over again till one understood it. She could not walk for joy; she ran, she trod on air. 'The swallow has set her six young on the rail,' she cried as she skimmed along. Then she drew a deep breath as another wave broke over her. What people these were! She had shared their enjoyment and the enjoyment had been open and unashamed. Too often the things she liked she had to like in secret, making excuses when she was found out. 'I enjoy painting,' 'I am very fond of reading,' – she put up these faint defences against being thought odd. But the Frasers were of her party. What was important to her was important to them. Against these people she needed no defence.

'For the lake, its swan;
For the dell, its dove;'

she chanted, bounding from the further stile. But in the silence of the woods her voice became small; the rest was too passionate to be sung aloud.

The kitchen passage smelled of roast meat. The servants were carrying dishes into the dining room. She ran up the back stairs without being seen and was able to change her wet shoes and stockings before anybody caught her. Nell came into her room with a piece of news. 'Aunt Carrie thinks it may be too stormy for calling this afternoon. Shall you mind if we don't go?'

'I'd be dead of joy, James Lee.'

Nell's pretty eyebrows stretched to a comic height.

'More Fraserisms?'

'Yes, yes, a great many more,' exulted Laura, dancing round her sister and waving stockings.

'Well, what did you do, my dear?' enquired her aunt at lunch. She was softening towards the Frasers.

'Oh, Aunt Carrie, we read poetry. Mrs Fraser read aloud.' Laura could not keep the eagerness out of her voice.

'Indeed,' graciously observed Mrs Young, 'that was a good occupation for a wet day.'

'George Fraser is a lucky man,' added her husband. 'His profession allows him to stay at home in wet weather.'

Nobody had anything to add to that, and so he turned the conversation by telling them of the death of an old man on the estate.

CHAPTER VI

'OLD RUDD is dead.' The remark was not irrelevant. Both nieces felt in it an indirect rebuke. Laura had been enjoying herself with her new friends at The Shrubbery; old Rudd had died in comparative neglect.

At one point the girls fell short of Mr Young's hope for them. He was disappointed by their unwillingness to 'visit'. Laura and Nell were disappointed in themselves; somehow they had never thought they would find it difficult.

'There must he something wrong with us,' declared Laura earnestly. 'We know so many people who enjoy visiting. Think of Grace Woods and that dreadful street in Penge. She used to go there twice a week.'

'Yes; but you know, Lolly, the Vicar found it for her when she was so in love with Mr Herbert. When he left and that spotty little curate took his place she got much less serious about it.'

'Oh, Nell!' Laura looked shocked at first, then the corners of her mouth trembled. Nell's suspicions coincided with her own.

'Anyway,' she added, 'Grace Woods did visit; and if she found it easy in Penge I don't see why we should find it hard in Norfolk. They are all Uncle's tenants and very friendly when we meet them. Only – '

'It's no good, Lolly; you know you hate it as much as I do. We can't understand what they're saying and we both feel impostors. I don't mind going if I've got a parcel to take or if there's a new baby, but to push in on old people whom we don't know and who have been here much longer than we have seems quite impertinent somehow and I really won't do it. And after all why should we go if Birdie enjoys going?'

Birdie made up in zeal for the girls' timidity. Brought up in a country rectory, visiting had no terrors for her; she spent all her spare time in charitable errands, and was already known in the village as 'the lady with the basket'.

'Though I hope they pay attention to what I say as well as to what I bring,' she protested, flushing proudly when Mr Young complimented her on her industry.

Nell was beginning to know the farm labourers because she often rode with her uncle when he made his morning rounds. Her mare, a charming well-mannered grey, was nominally shared by the girls, but it was usually Nell who went out. Laura was so vague and unpunctual that she often missed her turn.

Nothing at present mattered to Laura except her painting. She was so absorbed in it that she thought about it whenever her thoughts were free, and sometimes during carriage drives found her right hand twitching as her mind made imaginary strokes with the brush. She had never in her life before found so many subjects worth painting, nor had she ever worked so much at her ease.

It had soon become clear that the little sitting room with Nell's piano in it was not big enough for two people. Nell never interfered with her sister's belongings, but Birdie, called in to play accompaniments, made no bones of pushing the easel out of the way or moving brushes. She would sniff as she came in and grumble about the smell of paint.

'A smell is no worse than a noise,' Laura said one day. 'Nell sings "la-la-la" for hours and you don't mind.'

'A smell, if you must use that word, Laura, is worse to my mind than any noise. And even if it were not I should prefer to suffer the noise.'

'Why is that?'

'Because music is a greater art than painting.'

'How can you say so?' demanded Nell, up in arms for her sister.

'Music gives pleasure to a larger number. A singer can please hundreds at once while a painter pleases a few.'

'But a picture lasts for ever.'

'So does a musical composition.'

There seemed to be some flaw in the argument but Laura was too angry to find it. She banged the door instead on the opening notes of Balfe's 'Come into the garden' and stood in the passage wondering what to do. The sitting room was lost to her for the next hour, her aunt was downstairs and would want to talk, the maids were in occupation of the bedrooms. In despair she climbed to the third storey and discovered a retreat.

Beyond the servants' quarters the passage turned at right angles; a little distance down it there was a box room door. This room was long and low but not too full of lumber, with a good-sized window at the far end. And in the passage just opposite the box room door another window, facing south, gave enough light for painting if the door was left open, and created fascinating cross lights further inside the room. The turn of the passage hid her from the maids. Here was a place to work in undisturbed.

It was a wet day and she stood for a long time in the little passage, staring through rain-blurred panes at the green of the park. Then she pushed her way to the box room window and found that it looked out on the roof, a flat wet surface now shining grey as a sea, with plastered chimney stacks rising cliff-like from it. In the middle of this sea an encased bubble, the dome of the hall skylight, blocked her view. In fine weather she could easily climb out on the roof; she wondered if Nell had already explored it. But the dead butterflies on the window sill signified no such disturbance; even the maids, she fancied, seldom came in here. With a delicious feeling of freedom she began to move the furniture, cleared the rubbish from a couple of chairs and tilted upwards a stiff brass telescope on its mahogany stand to fit into the space behind the door. With a strip of carpet unrolled where she meant to put her easel the room made quite a presentable studio. She was certain her uncle would let her use it.

And with the discovery of the box room came another discovery that promised Laura more time for painting. The credit for the second find belonged to Nell; she was driven to making it through pity for her aunt. For there was no denying that the brougham was uncomfortable: the springs were bad and seats too wide and high. The most carefully stuffed cushions jolted out of place and a drive of any distance brought on backache. The ladies at present went out every day returning calls and every day found Mrs Young increasingly peevish. She would have liked to postpone some of the visiting, but her husband was punctilious in social matters and insisted on their going out whenever the weather allowed. As he himself escaped most of the calling the others felt the more reason to grumble. Mr Young was not indifferent to his family's sufferings, but he was a man who liked his possessions to meet his exact requirements and would undergo any discomfort while waiting to achieve his end. The Norwich coach-builders he first tried proved argumentative and slow; he had left them and gone to a London firm. The carriage he meant to have would take a long time to make; meanwhile his wife and nieces must make do.

One day Nell came back from the stables bubbling with excitement. She found her uncle in his study and at once began her attack.

'Uncle, have you forgotten the basket carriage? Thrower says it was built for Grandfather. It is very comfortable.'

'It is. Your grandfather used it till he became too feeble. I sold the ponies only a couple of years ago.'

'Thrower says he knows a lady who would sell us another pair. He thinks it would be a bargain to buy them.'

Mr Young looked up from his letters and laughed. 'Nell, I can see where this conversation is leading me. But, my dear, if I bought these ponies the phaeton would still be too small. Remember, the third seat was taken out to make room for your grandfather's leg rest. With your aunt and a man to drive her, there'd be no room for you and Lolly.'

'I thought perhaps I might learn to drive. Thrower thinks I could manage a pair.'

He looked at her eager face with approval. 'I believe you could. But your aunt would never consent.'

'Dear, dear Uncle, if you buy the ponies I promise I will manage Aunt Carrie.'

The ponies were a stolid pair, obstinate but reliable. As Thrower said, they could have driven themselves. Mrs Young, brought to the door one afternoon by Laura, looked horrified when she saw Nell handling the reins. But she hesitated a second before refusing a drive, and so her husband coaxed her to take a little turn.

'Just out of one gate and in at the other,' she said. 'Nell, please understand I don't want to go far.' Nell gave a wink at her uncle as they started off. They were gone for almost an hour.

Laura heard them coming back and ran out to the porch. They clattered up in fine style and stopped smartly beside her. Nell's curls were flying, her cheeks pink. Mrs Young was beaming. The drive had been a complete success.

'Such a nice afternoon. Nell drives very well. The Gordons passed us and stopped to compliment her.'

'And you were comfortable?'

'Oh yes, very. Indeed I feel quite sorry to get out.'

Laura learned to drive too, but her aunt had no confidence in her. When she went out she preferred to be driven by Nell. This suited both girls, for Nell loved society, while Laura was always glad of an afternoon to herself.

There were not many such afternoons however. Invitations assailed them now from every side. With a delicate aunt and an absentee uncle the girls till they came to Norfolk had led quiet lives, and they entered strange houses with as much apprehension as pleasure. As they were still in mourning, however, their engagements were small and informal, and they often found themselves within earshot of one another at table, sometimes near enough for mutual help.

'What were you talking about to that funny fat man?' asked Laura. 'You kept him going for such a long time.'

'We were talking of fishing,' said Nell demurely.

'But Nell dear, you don't know anything about fishing.'

'Lolly, he never found out.'

The next day Laura had similar luck discussing church architecture with a clergyman, and from this grew up the game of Fortunate Topics. Each sister had to notice how long she could keep her partner engaged on a single subject and to report the subject to the other. If both had lit upon the same topic, either could use it again another time. But if one had been blessed with remarkable inspiration that topic was exclusively hers, unless she chose to sell the rights. Laura bought Fishing from Nell with a roll of ribbon and some safety pins. Nell very much wanted to buy Tenants' Cottages from Laura, but Laura was pluming herself on her find and refused at present to sell.

'I don't care,' said Nell after some unsuccessful teasing. 'You can keep it; I think it's dangerous. It's just the subject to make old men ask if Uncle is sound. Then we have to explain that he is a Liberal and after that we get scolded for our uncle's good. I never like to console them by saying that he's not sound either way.'

'What do you mean?' cried Laura, properly scandalized at last.

'Well, it was not till Uncle told us that morning about his education that I began to understand his politics. Haven't you ever noticed how proud he is of being a Liberal, as if it were something rather difficult to be? That's because he is only a Liberal by education. I'm sure you have to be born to it to feel comfortable.'

For all the amusement they got by going about together the unsociable Laura soon became bored. The fuss of getting ready, the long slow meals, the dull waiting in drawing rooms seemed to her too much to pay for very little enjoyment. She knew her partners at table found her difficult to talk to, and she envied Nell who opened like a flower in the certainty of pleasing and being pleased. Nell grew prettier and more assured every time they went out. At Oakley Court she was a great success.

Their host, Sir Edward Hawley, was an important local landowner, with a voice in county affairs. More people than usual had been invited to meet them at lunch. Laura could not see Nell from where she sat, but she heard a flow of laughter from Nell's part of the table and wondered what topic her sister had found to keep her partners amused. She herself was badly off, having on one side a schoolboy who blushed whenever he spoke, and on the other an elderly colonel, rather deaf. He asked her, as they all did, how she liked Norfolk, and then turned his entire attention to his plate.

Lunch went on, the room grew hot. Laura felt thirsty and her glass was assiduously filled. She would be sleepy in the drawing room afterwards, she thought; she was even drowsy here in this big ugly room, for the blinds had been pulled against the glare and the smell of fruit and flowers was overpoweringly strong. An old man told a long slow cricketing story; Sir Edward looked at his wife and told something racier. Ned Hawley egged his father on, but there came a sudden pause as Lady Hawley signalled to Mrs Young. It was a relief to get up from the heavy chairs. The rich table was spoiled, its fine array gone, fruit skins littering the dessert plates and wine glasses dotted awry. Everybody seemed a little flushed and untidy; the cool air of the hall blew refreshingly in.

Rose Hawley took charge of Nell and Laura. She was Laura's age but a good deal more sophisticated; she had spent a season in London and was openly regretting that her father would not take a house again this year.

'I shall stay with my grandmother for some weeks,' she said, 'but of course that will not be so nice.'

'Oh no, of course not,' agreed the sisters politely.

They seemed inclined to listen further, so Rose took them upstairs to her own boudoir and showed them her embroidery. She worked in coloured silks, unusually well, and Laura exclaimed her delight at the designs.

'I am sure you must do beautiful things yourself,' said Rose with gracious interest.

'I'm afraid I'm very clumsy. My work is all knots.'

'Oh no, you must be good, I'm positive. You have such taste.'

Laura looked uncomfortable and Nell explained, 'Lolly can't sew. She likes painting. And if she isn't painting she reads and reads and reads.'

'Oh dear, she must be very clever, I'm sure.'

Ned Hawley, tall and fair, had come up to join them and was fidgeting about the room. At last he broke out, 'Why are we wasting the fine weather? There's no one on the croquet lawn. Let's go down and play.'

He fussed over balls and hoops and was assiduous in finding a mallet for Nell. 'We are to play together,' he said when he had arranged it all. 'What colour will you be?'

'I'll be blue.'

'Capital,' he said, as if she had said something clever. 'Rose, Miss Nell Young will be blue.'

He admired Nell and was confident of being admired in return. Laura boiled with rage at his assurance and at the amazing duplicity of Nell. Nell could not possibly like anyone so stupid and conceited, and yet she was behaving as if she did. Not a word passed between the sisters, but they glanced at each other almost like strangers as the game went on. Nell became Ned's defender, Laura his enemy.

'I'll show her,' thought Laura with satisfaction when she saw that the elegant young man was the weakest player of the four. Presently her antagonism began to affect him and he left a position in front of a hoop to drive her further off.

'Be careful where you send her. My sister's a demon when her eye is in,' warned Nell.

'Light punishment this time,' declared her partner, and he rashly left the red ball in a good place on the ground. It looked far enough away, but when Laura's turn came with a great swing of her mallet she made red knock black to the other side of the lawn, and completely out of position.

After that the game became a duel, Ned attacking persistently and a little wildly till Rose at last said, 'Do leave us alone. You can't beat Miss Young. She's playing like a wizard and you're deserting your partner simply to tease us.'

'Miss Young and I have accounts to settle and my partner doesn't mind. She plays a very pretty game on her own.'

'No, I don't mind. He can settle with Lolly,' laughed Nell, driving blue through a hoop and going on.

'Well, it's my turn to settle now,' cried Laura fiercely, and she hit black again by an astonishing fluke and then drove it deliberately off the grass.

Nell looked embarrassed, and Ned in some annoyance went off to rake among the laurels for the ball. Sounds of amusement reached Laura's ears, and she turned to find her uncle and some of the older men watching. Mr Young had come to warn them that the carriage was ordered. She reddened at being discovered in a temper and went indoors feeling ashamed of herself.

Nell said that evening, 'Why were you so cross, Lolly? I thought you'd break your mallet with that last stroke.'

'I hated that drawly voiced Ned; he annoyed me. I don't know why you were so nice to him.'

'He was nice to me. He would have been to you if you had let him. I didn't think he was so bad.'

'Nell, I believe you liked him.'

'Yes, I think I did.'

'But he was so conceited.'

'Oh well, it didn't matter.'

Laura went upstairs to brood in her bedroom. Now that Nell was grown up their lives might run less happily. She had noticed that Nell did not always like her friends, but it had never occurred to her that she might not always like Nell's. And what if Nell should choose to marry some man like Ned Hawley, a man of whom her uncle and aunt would certainly approve, whom only Lolly, fighting alone, could find any fault with? She determined, if such a plan were ever set afoot, that she would write at once to Henry Armstrong. It would be a proper occasion for asking his help. So strong was her determination that she got out the little writing desk he had given her and looked up his address. Henry Armstrong had known them both since they were children in India. He was in India still, but Laura fancied he would shortly be due for home leave.

CHAPTER VII

NELL soon became a pet of the Hawleys. She drove to Oakley every week for lessons with Rose's singing master and often stayed on afterwards to lunch. At other times she arranged to practise with Rose. They were learning duets together.

Now Laura found herself able to visit The Shrubbery, and the Frasers in their easy way let her come and go as she would, realizing without comment that she was less free than they. Their unconventionality pleased her; even their poverty and untidiness had its charm. She saw them living happily in circumstances that she had been taught to suspect, and she fancied that the current of their lives flowed more strongly because unencumbered. Every visit gave her something to remember, either instructive or absurd. Once she found the schoolroom floor laid over with paper patterns, the women crawling about with mouths full of pins while James read out the instructions in the fashion book. Another day she listened to a children's story and joined in the rookish clamour for more when Mr Fraser stopped. And she spent the whole of one hot afternoon helping catch the ponies that Rob and little Katy had let escape. Then for the first time she saw the poet angry; but she was the only one whom his outburst shocked. These recollections were not in themselves remarkable but they glowed in contrast with the frigidity of Yule Lodge.

By degrees she lost her awe of Margaret. Margaret never quite forgot her college standing nor the advantages of being older than her friend, but Laura felt none the less that she was glad of her companionship; by her own confessing she was lonely in her father's house.

'Will you live at home when you leave College?' asked Laura one day, looking forward to a time of uninterrupted friendship.

'Oh no,' exclaimed the other, almost vehemently, 'I shall probably teach, but I would like to do something very great and important – rule a kingdom, perhaps, or be a prime minister.'

They both laughed.

'You long to be famous yourself if your father is famous,' said Margaret. 'People turn to stare at me because I am George Fraser's daughter. I want them to stare at me because I am myself.'

Laura glanced at her with admiration and Margaret went on boldly, as if it eased her to out with the truth. 'And after all, though I love being at home, I am not needed there. My father and stepmother think more of each other than of anyone else in the world. Esther reads all he writes, you know, and tells him what she thinks of it. And if a manuscript is messy she copies it out. The house is always at sixes and sevens if a book is going away.'

'You might have had a cruel stepmother,' suggested Laura.

'Oh yes, I know. And I love Esther; nobody can help loving her, she is so good. But she is too unworldly. She would give away everything she had if we let her, and she spoils the children dreadfully because she can't believe they are naughty.'

'Does it distress your father?'

'It distresses me much more. They will get better presently, of course; James is beginning to look after Esther as we all do; he is a good boy. But Robbie and Katy are too little to understand and just now Rob is very difficult. He is not strong, you know, and everybody spoils him.'

She sighed, looked at the afternoon sun, and remarked, 'I ought to go home. There is nobody but Bessy today to help Esther put the children to bed.'

She did not stir from where she sat and Laura made no movement to break the spell. They were both green-elbowed from lolling in the grass; they had come out early meaning to paint but had settled in the corner of a field instead and talked and talked and talked. Blackbirds hopped in the grass near them, their yellow bills and anxious eyes just showing above the green; in the distance horses flicked their tails by a pond and here the swifts were swinging round the elms, up and round with a flickering of wings and then swooping down screaming for another half circle. The barn roofs they had come to paint showed through the trees; but an opulent curve of hedge shut the girls away from criticism, and against a stile near them pressed the hay of the next field, a tender barrier lulling their consciences.

'Tell me some more about your painting lessons,' said Laura, and Margaret lay back again in the grass. She loved instructing but did not always find a hearer and Laura was not as interested in tales of college life as Margaret would have liked her to be. The first respect paid to her as a learned woman had lessened when Laura discovered that Margaret was not in residence, but walked to Bedford Place every day from her godmother's house and lived a normal life with a large family of cousins at such times as she was not attending classes. The hours of work, the struggle to keep up, sounded praiseworthy rather than romantic. Once they had been described there seemed nothing left to tell.

But to stories of the art school Laura felt she could listen for ever. She was almost angry when she discovered that Margaret followed the courses less for the sake of painting than because she had been persuaded by a certain Miss Baldwin.

'The school is a long way off – in Knightsbridge,' said Margaret with an air of confession. 'And it is expensive; I couldn't ask my father. But my godmother discovered how much I was longing to go and she very kindly pays my fees. It is a good school, of course, the best artists visit it. During my first term Mr Millais was a visitor. I remember how surprised I was when Chloe asked him questions.'

Margaret's answers too often led to Chloe Baldwin; today

Laura wanted to hear about other things.

'I should like to go to a school too,' she said. 'I should like to know about pictures as well as paint them. For instance, when is a picture perfect? Mr Woodward used to say, "When you can't improve it", but that's really not a good definition. Suppose you had put in enough but not too much, suppose in fact you were an artist of genius and yet your picture did no good to any one who looked at it. Would it be perfect then?'

'A faultless picture would do good somehow.'

'You think so? So do I, but it's hard to prove. I went with my painting class to the Grosvenor Gallery and when I saw The Golden Staircase I almost cried for joy. But my friend Grace Woods – she is very downright, you know – said it couldn't be a great work because it had no message. Those girls were only there to please the artist's fancy; nobody was the better for looking at them. We went on arguing till she said that a badly painted picture with a good meaning might do more for a person who looked at it than a gallery full of Burne-Jones. Of course, that argument is absurd, but I can see that the best thing is to have good painting in a noble picture. But how does one achieve nobility in pictures? How does one achieve it in writing either? It isn't always to be found in stories about good people; and that is curious when you think of it. Do they solve problems for you at your art school?'

'Not at mine,' confessed Margaret. 'But I wish you could argue with Chloe. She worries over things like that.' Then she added importantly, 'You ought to read Aristotle.'

Laura felt ignorant and looked embarrassed.

'Aristotle was a Greek philosopher. We were reading his *Poetics* last term and we came across a lot about painting.'

'But I can't read Greek.'

'Oh, my father has a translation. I think I can lend it you if you will come back to the house.'

They picked up their things and sauntered across the fields to The Shrubbery. But when they turned the corner of the drive Mrs Fraser signalled so violently from the schoolroom window that Margaret turned pale. Saying 'I told you so; something's wrong,' she ran ahead to the house. Laura followed through the glass doors and found herself in a scene of great distress. The room was untidier than she had ever known it. Children's toys covered the floor and the entire contents of a nursery medicine chest – bottles, spoons, glasses, a syringe and night-light containers – had been set out on the window sills. Just under the window Robbie lay on the sofa. His mother kneeling beside him turned a desperate look on the girls; her hair was slipping from its net, her face was white. The small boy opened his eyes as his sister came in, then shut them and rolled up the balls in a horrible way. James at a distance stood staring stonily. The gaping maidservant held Katy.

'What's the matter?' cried Margaret. 'What has Robbie been doing?'

'He was playing hospitals with Katy; James was with me. They got at the medicine chest – I don't know how they reached it – and when I came in I found the belladonna gone.'

'Did he take it?'

'He won't say.'

'What does Katy say?' Margaret turned to her little sister but the child hid her face in Bessy's apron and started crying. 'There, there,' said the girl, patting her mechanically but never taking her greedy eyes off the white-lipped boy.

'She says he took it and made dreadful noises. In fact, he frightened her so much that she ran out to find me. But James thinks he is pretending all the time.'

'What does belladonna do?'

'I don't know. It's a poison.'

The women stared at each other in horrified ignorance and the servant girl gulped noisily. Margaret glanced at her elder brother, then came briskly forward and took the small boy's hand. His face every minute grew more white and pinched, his eye sockets were hollow, all his joints limp. It seemed impossible that he could be acting, and yet Margaret looked only half alarmed.

'I don't believe he took much if he took any at all. His hands are cold but they feel all right and his feet are quite warm. Let's get him upstairs and put him to bed. You go, Bessy, and turn it down.'

The maid reluctantly left the absorbing scene and Margaret turned to the elder boy. 'James, saddle the pony and hurry off for the doctor. You'll probably catch him just coming home. Tell him what's happened: say that Robbie meddled with the things in the cupboard and needs a very strong dose. You'd better ask him to bring the black stuff he brought last time.'

'I'll tell him,' said James with fervour, beginning to put on his boots. For some reason he was in stockinged feet.

'Now for hot bottles.' And Margaret moved to the door. As she left the sofa her little brother began to sob.

'Darling,' said Mrs Fraser, bending over him.

'Don't tell the doctor,' whimpered the child.

'But Robbie dear, you must have something if you took that nasty stuff.'

He rolled towards her in an agony of tears. The movement was confession enough and Mrs Fraser caught him up with a great sob of relief. There was an instant's silence as the two locked fast, Robbie's face in his mother's neck, her arms rocking him. 'Oh Robbie, why – ' began Mrs Fraser, but at the quiver in her voice Laura turned away. Witnesses had become intruders here and she followed Margaret into the hall. James, one boot off, came out after them, his face screwed up in comical resignation. 'He won't be punished, you'll see,' he told them darkly. And then he hopped away on one leg down the stone-flagged passage.

Margaret went away and came back with two handsome leather-bound volumes. 'I'm sure Father won't mind my lending you these. Skip the first pages if you find them difficult. The interesting part begins somewhere in Book IV.'

Laura admired Margaret for remembering her promise in circumstances so alarming and bewildering, and when she was in bed that evening she lit a candle, determined to do justice to the loan by beginning it at once. But, though the old-fashioned type, the footnotes, the frequent italics and capital letters roused her curiosity, she found herself thinking all the time not of Aristotle but of Mrs Fraser. Robbie hurt his mother because he loved her, chose her to hurt because he loved her most of all. Yet, the naughtiness over, he clung to her and was forgiven in an ecstasy that ignored spectators. The tenderness of the scene pierced Laura's tranquillity. Even when she blew out the candle and lay down she felt restless and turned over several times before she went to sleep.

In the morning nothing of this remained. She woke with a longing to taste her new book. But there were the usual delays: she had flowers to do for Birdie, notes to write, even dress materials to discuss with her aunt. Mrs Young, hesitating between spot and pinstripe, called everyone in to help her decide. It was three days later before Laura had time for Aristotle, and then she marched up to the box room in a lofty mood, taking notebook and pencil along with her two heavy volumes.

She settled herself on cushions in a seat under the window and arranged her possessions conveniently round her. Sunshine blazed across her feet, a breeze rattled the blind cord, far below and out of sight a garden-roller groaned, and distantly from another part of the house she could hear the piano. Rose had come over to practise with Nell.

'Aristotle in the attic,' she said to encourage herself, to make herself feel important before she began. She could not really believe that she would understand or enjoy the book, and when she set to work it was righteously, as on a task. She skipped through the first part as Margaret had said she might, and then began to read with close attention.

The blind cord went on rattling, the sunlight shifted, and presently Laura looked up with startled eyes. 'But I am enjoying this,' she whispered in a curious excitement and she fell upon the book again with such eagerness that she could feel the tips of her ears grow hot. She read absorbedly – but not as she read novels, and every now and then she would stop to think. First, she stared out of the window, then she frowned at the floor, finally in her wrestling she walked about the room. But when she flung herself down to devour more, the outside bell rang and soon after it the first gong and she knew that the morning was over. She shut the book, shook out her crumpled skirts and walked downstairs, feeling that her life had changed. She had read Aristotle and had enjoyed it. Nothing could ever be the same again.

Rose stayed to lunch and was pretty and vivacious. In hot sunshine they drove out to take her back. Then they went on to pay some other visits, but neither family called on was at home. They drove back quietly to tea in the drawing room, Birdie came in to pour because Mrs Young was tired. The blinds were drawn against the heat, the room was dusk and mellow, bright lines shone on the tea table silver. Laura drank from a white cup spotted with rose buds, thin gold lines round handle and rim. She ate bread and butter, she ate cake; everything was as usual but nothing was the same. In a dream she heard the others talking, in a dream she left them after tea. She walked to the Frasers without knowing what she was doing; life became real again inside their gate. A wheelbarrow stood at the edge of the lawn and Margaret in gardening gloves was weeding a border.

'Margaret,' said Laura without preamble, 'I have enjoyed reading that book more than I can possibly say. I began this morning and stopped for lunch and I haven't dared think of anything else for fear of forgetting the questions I meant to ask you.'

Margaret looked startled and rather pleased. 'What do you want to ask?' she said, spreading a rug on the grass for Laura to sit on.

'Well, first, what does "transient and compendious" mean? It came just where I was beginning to enjoy the beginning. Aristotle said that to learn was a natural pleasure, not confined to philosophers but common to all men, only that ordinary people partook of it in a more transient and compendious manner. I learned it off by heart in order to ask you.'

'I expect it is a bad translation,' said Margaret after a pause. 'Twining is very often misleading.'

'Then you can't tell what Aristotle really said?'

'Not unless you can read the Greek.'

Laura looked so disappointed that Margaret added, 'Still, you can get a fairly good idea. Was that all you wanted to ask?'

'Oh no. The next piece was not hard, only sorrowful for us. Do you think he meant it when he said that women were usually bad rather than good, and slaves altogether bad? And if so, I suppose when he says that all men find pleasure in learning he means men and not women. Is that true?'

'My dear Laura,' said Margaret in her most grown-up manner, 'have you never read any Greek history? Women held such an inferior position in ancient Greece that you need not distress yourself over what the philosophers say of them.'

She sounded convinced and Laura could not argue. She turned instead to a third problem. 'Well, Margaret, listen to this. This is the most difficult of all. Why should the end of life be action of a certain kind, not quality? And what is the difference between an action and a quality?'

'Oh Laura, you are taking this very much to heart. Let's go and talk to father; he will explain.'

They found the poet in his favourite attitude, lying back in a long chair with his feet on a stool. They came across the lawn so softly that he was not aware of them till they sat with a flop of their skirts on the grass by his side.

'Laura and Margaret,' he murmured without turning his head. 'You have something to ask me; I can tell it by your walk.'

'Mr Fraser, please will you give me your advice?'

'With pleasure, my dear Laura. State your problem.'

'Well,' Laura drew a breath, 'Birdie says – '

'Is that the little woman with the basket? A good name for her. What then says Birdie? A little bird told me – '

'Oh Father, do listen. We want you to be serious.'

'Child, I will be serious. Laura, speak.'

'Well, then – Birdie is my old governess and she has always said Duty First, Pleasure Afterwards. And if I hated books and had to read them, Birdie would call it duty. But as I love reading, other things become duties and it seems better for me to hem pinafores for a mission than to sit upstairs with my books. At least, that's what Birdie thinks. I have always felt she was wrong somehow, though I couldn't explain why, but this morning I read in Aristotle – '

'Aristotle, eh?' Mr Fraser looked surprised.

'I lent her your Twining, Father. She promised to take care of the books.'

'H'm.'

Was he angry? Laura shot him an imploring glance. 'I put them into brown paper covers at once,' she said.

His mouth twitched. 'You may borrow from my library whenever you like. Margaret knows quite well she ought not to have lent Twining without permission, for I am extremely particular about certain books. But you may have carte blanche as long as you tell me what you are taking. Is that clear?' There was such gratitude and relief in her face that he added quickly, 'Don't stop to make speeches, but tell me word for word what Aristotle says.'

Laura paused, then recited with Twining's emphasis: 'Happiness consists in action, and the supreme good itself, the very *end* of life, is *action* of a certain kind, not *quality*.'

'Well remembered. Now tell me, how does that apply to you?'

'As far as I can make out, sewing is an action and reading the *Poetics* is more likely to be a quality.'

'I should call both of them actions. Reading needs an expenditure of energy.'

'Then how can I decide which is the more important?'

'Perhaps you might consider the final end. You wish to acquire knowledge; your savages may not wish to acquire petticoats.'

Laura looked so blank that Margaret helped her. 'He means the missionary clothes you are making.'

'Oh,' she explained, 'they're not for savages. They're for female orphans in a home.'

Mr Fraser shouted with laughter. He laughed for some time while the girls sat waiting. At last he looked down very kindly at Laura. 'Listen, my dear. We all come to a point at which we have to decide for ourselves. We may even have to dispute the opinions of our old governesses. But if those governesses have brought us up well we shall, on the whole, desire the things that are good. And remember that after a certain age nobody but yourself knows what is really good for you. You have come to me for advice, Laura. Here it is. Action is the end of life, reading Aristotle is a worthy action, and Margaret will not always be here to help you read. While you may I should spend as much time on it as you can without offending your old governess or letting your female orphans go unclad.'

'Then I think I'll go straight back to my book.'

She stood up and held out her hand. He pulled himself out of his chair and put both his on her shoulders. 'Let me know,' he said, 'when you have more problems to solve.'

CHAPTER VIII

MARGARET came to look at the passages in Twining and as they sat together in the box room she suddenly blushed and said, 'Do you know, I am sure I could teach you Greek.'

'Teach me?' Laura caught her excitement and kindled. 'Could I really learn?'

'Of course, if you don't mind the drudgery. There is a lot to get by heart at first, you know.'

'I could manage that, I think.'

'Then why don't you try? You would be interested.'

'Interested? I should love it. But listen, Margaret,' Laura jumped from her seat and began to pace up and down the strip of carpet. 'If I learn, it must be properly. You must come to me or I must go to you for a definite number of hours every week, and you must charge me just what a master would charge.'

'Oh, no. I didn't mean that. I couldn't: I don't know enough. Really, Laura, I only meant to teach you for fun.'

'But don't you see that proper fees will make all the difference? If you come as a friend nobody here will believe I am learning seriously, and Greek will give way to any other plan. But if I ask Uncle to pay for a set of lessons, then the lessons will become important, and Aunt Carrie and Birdie will know that I shall not be free at certain hours.'

Margaret saw the position. 'But will your uncle approve?'

'Oh yes, I am sure he will. Nell is very much taken up with her singing just now, and it seems reasonable for me to want lessons of some sort too.'

Mr Young, however, was not so quickly persuaded.

Something in the suggestion displeased him, though Laura found it hard to discover what.

'Greek, my dear Laura, what good will that be to you?'

'I don't know that it will be any particular good. I should be able to read Greek quotations when I found them in books.'

'Well, that is something, certainly. But it hardly seems a sufficient reason.'

Laura thought a moment and than reminded him, 'You didn't object to my learning Latin.'

'You were a child then. Now you are a young lady with other occupations. Are you sure Margaret Fraser has not persuaded you into this?'

'Oh no, Uncle; I want to learn. It was my idea that she should give me regular lessons so that I should work more steadily.'

'I am glad you realize you are undertaking no trifle. But don't you think you may spend too much time on what is perhaps a fad?'

Laura blushed, remembering crazes of the past that had ended suddenly.

'Margaret is so sensible, Uncle. I don't think she would let me give up too soon.'

'But why begin if you are not sure of yourself? If you had never met Margaret Fraser you might not have thought of this. I like the Frasers as a family, I am glad you and Margaret have made friends; but I would prefer you to make other friends as well, Laura. You allow yourself to be engrossed by some people and to be too critical of others. Would not Nell agree that I am right?'

'I suppose so, Uncle.' His cool, remote tones frightened her. He kept himself too well in hand; not angry, only grieved, he chose from a safe distance, god-like, the tender place to strike. Silence was her only refuge; she sat staring at the carpet. It was no good going away with an unanswered petition.

He realized she was waiting and began a new attack. 'A

little while ago you were talking of painting lessons. Have you already changed your mind about those?'

This was hypocrisy. He knew she would never change. With a spurt of impatience she steadied her voice to reply 'No; I would very much like to have lessons in September. But while Margaret is here and can teach me Greek I should like to learn that. I certainly don't mean to give up painting for Greek.'

'Very well, my dear, if you think you will enjoy the drudgery – ' He shrugged his shoulders and turned to his writing table again.

Laura had won permission; but she knew as she left him that he had given way only because she had reminded him that Margaret would presently go back to College.

After this battle it was easy to face Nell. But Nell for once made no attack.

'Well, Lolly darling, if you want to learn Greek I don't see why you shouldn't. Every man to his own poison.'

'But why should Uncle be suspicious of Margaret Fraser?'

'I expect he feels as I do. She's so putting off. She always has plenty to say to you but when anyone else comes in she stops talking as if what she was saying was too deep for ordinary ears.'

'I am sure she doesn't think that. She is just shy.'

'Well, it looks more like bad manners. Or perhaps a sort of conceit, as if she were a missionary chatting to her convert but keeping at a distance all the obstinate heathen. It's no good pretending you're not amused, Lolly. I can see your face in the glass.'

After this Nell was delighted to find Margaret delivered into her hands before the first lesson. Margaret came earlier than Laura expected and was shown into the drawing room where Nell was strumming. Nell immediately offered to take her upstairs and they found Laura improvising a table in the box room.

'Here's your tutor,' announced Nell with suspicious heartiness, then looked round for some mischief to do. Shah had taken a fancy to the box-room window sill and he now strolled in behind the girls. 'Oh, the darling,' cried his mistress, 'he wants to learn Greek too. Margaret, will he worry you if he stays? He can listen very nicely from the window sill.'

'I am sure he won't disturb us,' said Margaret primly. She was never quite at her ease in Nell's company.

'Then if he catches flies would you mind letting Lolly stop him? She needn't watch, of course; she must simply listen for the pounce.'

'Nell,' said her elder sister, 'please take your pet away. I've no intention of looking after him.'

Nell slowly gathered up the cat and dawdled into the passage. Margaret unstrapped her books and took off her hard straw hat. She was still shy and her manner was self-important. Nell's grimace as she closed the door spoke volumes to her sister.

When the latch had finally clicked Laura felt much relieved. 'I hope you don't mind coming up here,' she said. 'Nobody will disturb us, and in the other rooms we are never safe. Everyone thinks me mad for liking to sit amongst boxes, but I assure you I have good reason.'

Shyness vanished as the lesson began. The letters of the Greek alphabet delighted Laura and she drew them with a fine steel pen, neatly and still more neatly, till Margaret grew tired of her childishness and took her on to the grammar.

At the end of the hour Laura said dismally, 'We can't meet again till Thursday. What shall I do till then? I shall get on too slowly if I don't work by myself.'

With the face of a person putting someone else to the test Margaret marked four pages in the dog-eared book. 'Don't do all this if you can't manage it,' she said. 'Do some of the declensions and some of the verbs. The chief thing is to be word perfect: whatever you learn, please learn it thoroughly.'

She evidently set more than she expected Laura to master and she was astonished at their next meeting when her pupil, hardly hesitating, recited all four pages without mistake.

'Well,' exclaimed Margaret, shaken from her superiority, 'Laura, you have an amazing memory.'

'Ah, if you had seen me taught by Birdie you would know why I can learn by heart. But I admit I took pains over this. I have been getting up early on purpose to finish, and I propped the book on my dressing table last night and went through everything again before I got into bed. Now don't let's waste a minute, I'm longing to get over the dull part.'

But Margaret said slowly, 'You make me feel ashamed.'

'Do I?' cried Laura, delighted.

'I could never learn like that. But Laura, you also frighten me. You rush at things so – at books, at painting. Everything seems so important to you.'

'Don't you find things important too?'

'Not to such an alarming extent.'

Laura laughed and turned on to the next page. Margaret came regularly for the next few weeks and was prouder and prouder of her pupil. At last their pace began to slacken, as the box room grew stuffy in the hot weather. One morning they found they could bear it no longer; Laura pushed up the window and they climbed out on to the leads and settled in the shade of a chimney stack. Even when the sun came round they were not unpleasantly hot. Up here they felt every stirring of the breeze. The glare bothered Margaret until Laura crawled halfway back through the window and reached for an old carriage umbrella that lay along the top of the lumber. It was an enormous thing, of brown holland lined with green, with such a long handle that Margaret could prop it up and sit in its shade without having to hold it. The next day she brought a pair of dark spectacles with her and at the end of the lesson Laura said: 'Do stay as you are. I should like to paint you.'

'What, in black glasses, sitting like this?'

'You have no idea how well the sun shines on the umbrella. There is a light from the roof on your face and your spectacles shine splendidly although they are dark. Please don't take them off.'

Margaret was clearly unwilling to be painted in spectacles and Laura did not know how to tell her that they suited her. She noticed as she drew that Margaret looked better when her pale and rather short-sighted eyes were masked; as a result her mouth and finely moulded chin gained in significance.

She was an obliging model and at the end of a few days sketches for the portrait were successfully finished. Laura began to paint in a sort of ecstasy. The weather stimulated her; she loved the brilliant mornings on the roof top, which did not grow unbearably hot till noon. She was enjoying her Greek, a curious sense of power filled her when she looked at her exercise book and measured her progress. And she had an exhilarating sense of growing even with Margaret: she was sometimes the leader and Margaret the follower now. She enjoyed the Greek and Margaret enjoyed coming to see her. And it was Margaret who was the more disappointed if a lesson time was changed. Laura felt a slight contempt for this growing admiration, but it flattered her, made her more sure of herself and extremely alert. If Margaret had been what she and Nell called 'silly' Laura would have had no hesitation in sending her away. But Margaret was always so stolid and sensible, only a gleam sometimes betraying what she felt. And the Greek went on and the painting, and they chattered like sparrows in the intervals. Laura lived with all her energies during these morning hours.

When she was working on her picture she was hardly conscious of Margaret. Sometimes she made observations, then forgot what she had said.

'Your skin is so smooth and brown,' she found herself babbling. 'Margaret, I think you are rather like a fruit.'

'Sunflowers and fruit. What next, I wonder,' said Margaret, pretending not to care, though she looked pleased. Laura could not remember talking about sunflowers and was too much absorbed to ask. After a long pause she spoke again: 'You know, I haven't made you a bit pretty.'

'I don't mind.'

'You see, I haven't been painting you. I've been painting the light.'

'So I might just as well not be here.'

'Oh no – silly. But if I wanted to make a portrait of you I wouldn't give you a green face. At least, I don't think so.'

'Well, I hope not.'

But Laura did not answer. She was lost again in her painting and when she remembered Margaret next it was to say fervently, 'I think you are the most patient person that has ever sat for me.'

Margaret disclaimed the virtue. 'It's not patience; I enjoy myself. You amuse me, you're so odd.'

'Odd,' said Laura frowning at her canvas and pushing the hair back from her forehead with the back of her hand. 'So you think me odd.'

She was not attending but the word remained in her mind, and as she walked back with Margaret across the park she suddenly said: 'Margaret, am I really odd?'

'No, of course not. I was only teasing.'

'Are you sure? The first time you saw me, or that time when Mrs Fraser was reading poetry, are you positive you didn't think me odd?'

Margaret pondered, staring at the ground as she walked.

'No, I'm sure I didn't. I thought you pretty. So did Father; don't you remember how he made you talk?'

'Me pretty?' exclaimed Laura, extremely gratified. 'I'm not pretty; but Nell is.'

'Oh, she is lovely,' said Margaret warmly, and though Laura was glad to hear her sister praised she was sorry they had dropped the subject of her own looks so abruptly. She would have liked to hear more, but Margaret had forgotten what they were talking about and Laura had not courage enough to pick up that thread again. She reflected a little sadly that whereas when she was on the roof painting she was a sort of goddess who could make people do as she chose, out here on an ordinary level she was an undistinguished person ready to believe the worst of herself when others disapproved of her and glad to pick up the faintest crumbs of praise.

Margaret came early the next morning for a long sitting. The picture was so nearly finished that Laura was getting nervous. She had chosen a large canvas, longer than it was high, and had stood close to the subject so that the umbrella filled up most of the background, the sun brilliant on the cover, the lining a green gloom. Against this transparent shade came Margaret's pale face, her head bent slightly forwards and turned to the left, her dark glasses shining in the glare from the slates. The book propped on her knees showed above the lower edge of the picture and her washed-out holland dress with its quillings of white braid flowed away to the right, one fold just caught by the sunlight again. And here on the right Laura had brought the roof edge some yards nearer than it actually was, so that the green of tree tops showed below the green of the umbrella. It was the biggest and most ambitious picture she had ever painted.

Today she finished the folds of the dress and turned her attention to the face. At first she had meant to leave this almost blank but now with some hesitation she decided to try for a likeness: her picture should be a portrait as well as a study. But she began her attack too late, changed her mind, grew flurried, finally put down her brushes and walked away in despair. She found herself very near to tears: it was their last morning; tomorrow a visitor was due at the Lodge who would take up the whole of her time.

Margaret jumped up and came after her. 'Laura, don't worry. I can sit for you this afternoon.'

'That will be no good,' said Laura, keeping her back turned.

'Why not? Is there too much to do?'

'Hardly anything; but I can't paint when I'm feeling rushed.'

'Well, stop now and finish this afternoon. Will the light be too difficult?'

'No; I could manage.'

'Then what's the matter?'

'Nothing. I'm only feeling cross. I'm sorry.'

Margaret had the sense to go at once and Laura felt so

much better after lunch that she was able to excuse herself quite successfully from a drive that afternoon. Her uncle was out and her aunt made no objection, only expressing a hope that the picture would soon be finished since it was taking up so much of Laura's time.

Margaret came back. She was gentle and patient, and Laura was calmed by her sympathy. Margaret had the tolerance of a sensible children's nurse, accepting fractiousness as part of the natural plan. Laura sometimes wondered how far that kindliness would go: she could not easily imagine her angry or in tears.

Suddenly the picture was finished. Laura wiped her hands on a rag.

'Margaret, I'll show you the place I like best in the garden and then you shall come back to the roof and tell me just what you think of this.'

With great deliberation they walked downstairs and through the shrubbery to the kitchen garden door. Warmth and scent met them as they went in; the box edges smelt their sweetest in the afternoon sun. The men were working elsewhere and the great walled square was for once deserted. Bees hummed a loud reproach as they passed the lavender, a blackbird in the red-currant bushes squawked and darted away. The sun blazed on their backs as they stopped in front of a door; the key in the lock felt hot under Laura's hand. She did not turn it at once however but said over her shoulder, 'Just look back at the whole nice peaceful garden.'

'I see it.'

'Well then, you know the door we came in by. That goes back to the civilized house. Then there is another door in the stable wall. That takes you out to the potting sheds. There's still another one between the greenhouses. But that only leads to a ditch and the pond.'

'Well?'

'Now I'll show you what's behind this door. Stand back. It's very strange and special.'

She hitched the door up – it had sunk at one side – and

swung it open as she spoke. This fourth door of the garden opened straight into a wood. No path led between the close-locked trees; where the threshold ended the wood began. The trees however seemed to have drawn back a little from the doorway and the space so left was filled with a bed of nettles, young nettles, bright and a dangerous green.

'Is this your favourite place?' asked Margaret bewildered.

'Don't you like it?'

'No, I don't. It's frightening.'

'I'm so glad you think that. It frightens me too. It's like coming to the end of civilization. One thinks one is safe, and then one opens a door and finds this. I can only come here when I'm feeling fierce.'

'Are you feeling fierce now?' Margaret never knew. She was a faithful friend but always a little uncomprehending.

'Let's go,' said Laura. 'My picture's waiting.' She banged and locked the door, and they hurried back to the house. Laura whistled under her breath as they climbed the stairs.

She had not been mistaken. The picture was what she had thought it. She almost sang for triumph as she waited for the other to speak. Margaret was quite breathless. 'Laura, it's good, it's very good.'

'It's the best picture I have ever painted.' Her jubilation sought outlet. On a wave of pleasure she turned and kissed Margaret's warm round cheek.

To her horror Margaret blushed and looked positively uncomfortable.

'I'm so sorry,' cried Laura. 'I did that quite by accident.'

'I'm not sure,' said Margaret, rubbing her face, 'that your apology makes it any better.'

'Oh dear,' cried Laura, blushing in her turn. 'Please don't be cross, Margaret. I was so pleased with my picture I had to kiss someone.'

'You are so sudden,' complained Margaret. But then she added, 'Don't look so unhappy. Of course, I don't mind; I was only surprised.'

She began to talk about the picture and Laura tried to

answer her but the harmony of the afternoon had been broken and Laura wanted her to go away. She would not be able to think about her picture again till Margaret had gone, but she went down as usual to start her on the way home. They talked rather primly as they went and a hungry look came into Margaret's eye at the stile. But Laura avoided her glance, turned as if nothing had happened, and waved her a brisk and cheerful goodbye. On the way back however she let her pace slacken and whipped with a long bent of grass at the moon daisies, trying to shake off a feeling of guilt. Just as she reached the railings that divided park from garden her uncle came across the croquet lawn. Laura suddenly remembered that she was paint smeared and untidy and that he had no idea he would find her at home.

'Why Laura, I thought you were all out driving.'

'No, Uncle, I stayed at home to paint. Margaret Fraser came to let me finish her portrait. I had so little left to do and I wanted to make an end.'

'Well, upon my word, Laura. To paint indoors on an afternoon like this.'

Laura thought of explaining that she had been out of doors on a roof top, but he looked at her as if he found her in some way peculiar and she decided not to confess to further eccentricity. She was still conscious of the slight feeling of guilt that always made her uncomfortable in his presence. They had nothing more to say to each other and she went on into the house.

CHAPTER IX

LONG before Henry Armstrong arrived Rose was asking questions about him.

'Who is this man who is coming to stay? I really must know, you have talked about him so much.'

'He was a friend of Papa's,' said Nell to tease her.

'Oh, well,' said Rose.

But Henry was more than that. He was the girls' oldest friend and the only person who had known them at every stage of their lives. Laura connected him with her days in India: a young civilian in the District where her father's regiment was stationed, he had often come round to military lines to play with her and Nell. He was distantly related to their mother's family, and when they were orphans living with their grandmother in Sussex Henry had spent part of one leave with them. Laura by then was almost thirteen and Nell a dancing imp of eight. Henry became their devoted slave and playfellow, shocking the servants with the liberties he allowed, wheedling holidays and other treats for them from their grandmother.

The old lady was growing frail then, though the children did not notice it. The night before he left Henry called Laura into the garden while Nell was being put to bed. It was an autumn evening and already frosty; Laura could feel the chill of the ground through her thin shoes. They walked up and down the paths in the shrubbery and Henry told her he had something important to say.

'You are a big girl now, Laura. Will you remember?'

'I'll try.' She stared at him wide-eyed in the dusk.

'Listen, my dear. Your father was very good to me and your grandmother has always been kind. I should like in return for that to help look after their children, and as I am a connection of yours it is right that I should.'

'Are you one of our guardians?' She was proud of the ease with which the grown-up word slipped out.

'No. Your grandmother is one and your uncle is the other. You must always be a good girl and do as they say.'

Laura looked disappointed: no novelty in this.

Henry had gone on, floundering a little as if the going were hard.

'I am sure you will always be safe and happy; but suppose by some chance you were in distress – asked to do something you didn't want to do, uncertain over a choice. I would like you in such a case to know you could write to me. Laura, do you think you would remember to write?'

He spoke too earnestly; she felt uncomfortable. She scraped her toes on the gravel and screwed up her eyes. Henry bent over to peer into her face. 'Never mind, Laura dear,' he said quietly. 'Just try to remember; you can't quite understand. I've brought you a present, it's a little writing desk. And I've put my address on one of the ivory tablets so that if you want me you can write at once.'

They had only met twice since then. Once she stared at him dumbly across her aunt's tea table in Cheltenham, knowing from his expression that he guessed her to be unhappy but without any opportunity to talk to him alone. Another time he paid a flying visit to Bath to see them and found Laura prostrate with one of her severest headaches, hardly able to smile at him when he peeped through her bedroom door.

And now he was coming to stay at Yule Lodge. He had invited himself; Mrs Young announced the fact with irritating slyness. 'He says he wants to see you in your new home.'

'Does he?' asked Laura in an off-hand way.

Aunt Carrie paused, dismayed by this lack of interest, but

presently went on as her nieces knew she would: 'My dear, I hope you are not too much taken up with your lessons. Greek is all very well in its way but you have other things to think of. You must try to amuse your guest when he comes.'

'We don't amuse Henry, Aunt Carrie; he amuses us,' said Nell. 'Laura, do you remember his teaching us backgammon? I feel quite ready to play it again.'

But when Henry did come the old intimacy was not so easily renewed. He was shyer, more uncouth, than the girls remembered. He arrived at tea time; they were sitting in the drawing room and Mr Young went out to the hall when he heard the noise of wheels. 'Henry! My dear fellow – ' a bustling drowned the rest but the girls caught the growl of Henry's voice, which was lower than their uncle's. When at last he came into the room, stooping although the door was a high one, for he never held himself well, Laura was startled to see how much he had changed. Then she knew she was wrong: he had not changed at all, it was she who had forgotten what to expect. As he came round the door she anticipated every moment; this was just how Henry would walk and look. Even the incongruity of clothes and man was familiar; she must have accepted as a child what struck her so forcibly now. No clothes hung well on those long arms and legs, the fierce face rose surprisingly above an orthodox collar and tie. He was so shy that he glared at the girls as he shook hands with them; his bristling eyebrows had begun to curve downwards to his eyes. In face of his awkwardness Laura and Nell felt grown-up and self-assured, cool and charming in their pretty dresses. As children they had teased him for his jerky manners and gruffness, but the habits that amused them then now seemed almost a pity. He took a chair abruptly beside Aunt Carrie and she began to question him about his journey. Every time he answered Nell raked him with her eyes and Laura knew she was comparing him unfavourably with her uncle or Ned Hawley.

Henry looked more comfortable next day in very old clothes, but he still maintained a fierce reserve before the girls. For the first part of his visit he seemed determined to avoid them and the avoidance was made easier by Mrs Young's dislike. Henry was not at all Aunt Carrie's sort of man. Shy people made her uncomfortable and she complained that Henry had no gift for talk. Either he misunderstood what she was saying or he asked her questions which she could not answer. And he had other faults: he smoked too much, she could smell tobacco even when he had hidden his pipe. He had lived too long in uncivilized places; she was sure he had not been so difficult as a younger man. She avoided entertaining him by building up the theory that he was too much of a bachelor to enjoy feminine chat. Whenever he came into a room unaccompanied by her husband she gave him instructions for finding his host – adding to the instructions a look so full of meaning that Henry, convinced he was interrupting a conclave, would jerk for the door and leave the room to the women while Aunt Carrie sighed with relief and her nieces exchanged glances.

Mr Young however welcomed a guest and took Henry with him round the estate, visiting the farms and inspecting the cottages. The sound of their uncle's voice as he described and explained made the girls realize how quiet he usually was. As a rule he came in and went to his study without being noticed by the household. Now boots kicked the iron scraper and were brushed with vigour on the mat, men gave orders in the hall, flung keys on tables, tapped the barometer and rattled newspapers. The study door shut with a clap and then from behind it came a smell of tobacco, and their uncle's voice still expounding. The girls had no chance of meeting Henry properly; Mr Young was so pleased to have another man in the house that he kept him almost a prisoner. At meals the talk turned chiefly on coach building, as the landau was coming from London in a few weeks' time. The style of the carriage was new to Henry; he was willing to be impressed by description and by the coloured model on Mr Young's writing table.

From coach building the talk eventually drifted to politics, but by now the girls knew that their uncle was getting tired of his guest. The men's political opinions were opposed and merely gave Mr Young a chance to tease. Henry was solidly Tory, firm but inarticulate; round the dumb fortress of this obstinacy Mr Young flashed his batteries with considerable skill. His arguments stung if they did not convince. As a talker he was immeasurably the nimbler of the two.

'No Liberal gets in for a farming county,' grumbled Henry from the depths of an easy chair.

'It has been known,' his host assured him smoothly. 'Last year it happened in South Norfolk.'

'Must have been a fluke,' persisted Henry.

'By one vote, I admit; Read and Gurdon tied. On a recount they found a Conservative ballot paper scribbled with the name of the voter, so that paper was disallowed and Gurdon got in.'

'Don't you defeat youself by admitting all this?'

'Oh, I assure you, in the district my views are unique.' He stood smiling on the hearth rug, priest of a loftier religion, and Henry reddened slowly at his bantering note. 'Well,' he returned doggedly, 'I can't follow party politics in England. I can only see what is good for India and stick to that.'

Such an admission signalised defeat and the victor became magnanimous. Colonial opinion, Mr Young feared, was inevitably behind the times. Possibly Henry never saw the *Spectator*? 'Never,' said Henry, with immense decision, and he took up a book to avoid further argument.

Mr Young re-opened attack when the Frasers came to dinner. His wife rose in alarm as soon as he began.

'If the men mean to talk politics, let us leave them. They will have nothing further to say to us.'

But George Fraser growled, 'I'm not going to argue with you, Young. To vote Liberal in a farming county isn't politics, it's juggling. And I'm not skilful enough to juggle with you.'

Henry laughed and Laura as she left the room felt satisfied. Her tormented friend had found an ally at last.

Even Nell by now seemed to think Henry needed allies.

She suggested next morning that they should go for a picnic. 'Let's get Henry to ourselves for once, Lolly. At least, I suppose Birdie will come too, but she won't matter. Let's take tea with us and drive down to the mill. Henry will look so funny in the pony carriage.'

The seat removed from the phaeton was fitted in again and with Birdie squeezed between the girls there was just room for Henry with his back to the horses. He put one foot on the step in response to Nell's entreaties but took it off again before his weight was half up.

'I know you love to make a person look ridiculous, but just for this once, Nell, I'm not going to please you. If you three drive I'll cut across the fields and meet you.'

They had tea on the far side of the mill pond, watching the ducks in the distance and the miller's fair-haired children peeping at them round the corner of the house. After tea Birdie announced that she meant to visit the cottages, opened her parasol and set off across the field. When the prim little figure in its unbecoming dress had passed out of earshot embarrassment fell on the three left behind. Henry asked if he might light his pipe and leant back against the tree trunk stuffing the bowl. When he had got it going the tension relaxed and at last Nell looked at him with a challenge and said, 'Don't you think we've improved since you saw us last?'

His sudden smile was entirely friendly. 'Improved out of all recognition, I should say. I had quite forgotten I should find you young ladies.'

'Is that why you are so polite to us?' she went on teasing. 'In the old days you were never so polite. Do you remember shouting at me in Hindustani when I climbed a tree in Grandmamma's garden so high that I frightened you?'

Henry had forgotten, but Laura remembered. She and Nell had worn tartan frocks and button boots that morning. Henry took them out with him early after breakfast; they walked close either side of him on the garden paths so that each could hold a hand.

'I think that visit was the best I have ever paid,' said

Henry. The girls imagined he meant some compliment to them, but almost as if to conceal the possibility, he went on quickly, 'What became of your grandmother's old grey pony? He was such a friendly little beast, I remember.'

When Laura had recounted the fate of the grey pony, Nell, who was determined to bring the conversation back to the present, remarked, 'We are heiresses now, you know. Many people consider that an improvement too.'

It was just the remark to infuriate Henry. All the friendliness died out of his voice as he growled, 'Then I hope you realize your responsibilities. You, Nell, are not of age; but what about you, Laura? Do you know how much money you have and where it comes from?'

'The lawyer explained a great many things to me but I'm afraid I didn't understand them all. I just ask Uncle for money when I want it and if there is anything to sign he shows me where to put my name.'

'And what is the good of our knowing about money?' asked Nell. 'When we marry our husbands can manage it all.'

'Every woman ought to know the value of her property and to be interested in the disposing of it. How will you know what you ought to keep and what you owe to charity if you never have the disposal of regular sums?'

'Oh, but we do have that,' argued Nell. 'We have our dress allowance.'

'You see,' explained Laura, 'we go to Uncle if we want anything unusually expensive – Nell's singing lessons, for instance, or my Greek. But our dress allowances are supposed to cover the rest and out of them we save for benevolent objects. We have an old money box labelled B.O. and we put into it quite faithfully every week. In fact, the difficulty is not so much to save as to decide what to do with our savings. We sometimes positively hunt for an object for our benevolence. In the end we nearly always give the money to Birdie; she is sure to know of a mission or some poor person to help in the village.'

Henry laughed. 'This sounds more like old times. I don't believe you are so grown-up after all.' Then he added, 'And you're happy enough here as grand young ladies?'

Nell answered for both. 'I do very well, thank you; but Lolly has her ups and her downs. She would rather spend all her time on painting than on anything else in the world and she would much rather learn Greek than go out calling.'

'Ah,' said Henry, as he waited for Laura to speak. Suddenly she noticed that this was what he always did. Like the Frasers he expected her to have an opinion and uphold it; unlike the Frasers what she said would really matter to him.

'I would much rather paint than be sociable,' she admitted. 'Henry, does that strike you as being so odd?'

'Not in the least,' he answered firmly. 'Laura, I think our tastes are very much the same.'

They sat silent for a little. Then he persisted, 'But otherwise you enjoy being here?'

Again Laura hesitated and Nell turned to her boldly. 'Lolly, why don't you tell him about your dream?'

Laura blushed at being forestalled. She had determined to confide in Henry but wanted to choose the best moment for telling her tale. The thing was too important to be rushed at or mishandled; nothing would induce her to say more now. Henry saw her confusion and asked no questions but when Birdie came back he suggested that Nell should drive her home and let Laura walk with him. So it was arranged; they helped pack up the picnic and watched the others bump away over the grass. Then they took a footpath through the water-meadows, climbed the harsh slopes by the gravel pits, and so came out on a cart track across the fields. Here the going was easy; they walked side by side, Henry silent and Laura content. If he wanted her story she would not be afraid to tell it. He was a reassuring companion, she thought.

But he had something else in his mind. He suddenly looked down at her. 'Laura, you like Greek and that sort of thing. Would it make you happy to go with your friend to College? I fancy your uncle might disapprove of the plan at first, but he would let you go if you were set on it.'

In a flash she answered, 'I couldn't leave Nell.'

'Not even for that?'

'Oh no; we need each other. Though we sometimes quarrel we are really in league together, like the children of Israel in exile, you know.'

'And when you marry?'

'Then Nell will come and live with me. But I think she will be the first to marry. Then perhaps I might go to College; I could stay with her in the holidays.'

'She'll certainly marry.' He smiled as he thought of Nell. Then he asked Laura, 'Are you pleased with the way they have brought her up?'

'Well, they don't spoil her but they don't allow her to be as nice as she really is. As long as she is gay and pretty nobody minds what she thinks. I am the only person who knows what a darling Nell can be.'

He smiled at her in his nicest fashion. 'Now I shall find Nell and hear about you.'

Presently Laura told him the story of her dream. She flushed as she explained that it began with a nightmare, but Henry showed no amusement or surprise. He listened keenly throughout and when she had finished he strode on in silence for some time.

'Have you never said anything to your uncle?' he said at last.

She shook her head. 'He wouldn't think it mattered, you know. He would only say I was fanciful.'

'And are you still afraid?'

'A little,' she confessed. 'Partly because it was such a horrid dream – you have no idea how dreadful Nell's face was, looking in. And partly because I woke with such a feeling of guilt. It was something I had done that brought harm to Nell.'

'Then you still have the feeling that your dream may come true? I don't think it's likely that it will, you know.'

'I don't think it's likely, but I feel it's possible. That's what makes it all so serious for me. You see, Henry, I don't believe my dream foretells an unexpected accident, something as it were apart from myself. The ancient prophets foretold things like that, but one doesn't hear of the gift so often nowadays. I feel certain that my dream was a real part of me and that it may actually come true one day from some action of mine. And it may not even be an action I can understand or guard against; the everyday things I do may bring harm.'

'Laura, you mustn't let yourself be frightened.'

'Oh, I know, I mustn't be frightened and I mustn't get fussed. It is only when everything goes wrong – when I want to paint and Birdie scolds and Uncle disapproves that I get these headaches and horrible dreams. Then I become foolish and tiresome and let go of my good resolves; and it is when one lets go that the bad things come true.'

'It is,' said Henry. 'You are a wise little Laura.'

At the deep note in his voice she lifted her face and he met her look with a violence that made her feel shy. She remembered the evening long ago in her grandmother's garden when his earnestness had embarrassed her. Then she had screwed up her face and scraped her toes on the gravel; she was too old to do that now. But Henry was still as quick as before to read her expression; almost as she was recoiling from it the eagerness died in his face. Something unspoken trembled in the air between them but before she could catch the invisible words he was speaking of other things. He was not talking at random however; he had just turned over a page and was reading the end of a chapter of which the beginning had been suppressed.

'In September I go back to India again. The district I am in at present is not a good one – still unsettled and very hot all the year round. The married men don't bring their wives; it's no place for women. However I shall only be there for a little while longer; then I hope to get a good long leave.'

'Then you'll come back and see us,' suggested Laura, offering this to make amends for her failure of a minute before. His look warmed again, but they had reached the home farm and Nell was coming to meet them along the drive. He had only a few seconds more and he turned to her vehemently. 'Laura, I can't bear to think of your being unhappy, worrying and frightening yourself while I am away. Won't you write to me if it would help you? My dear, why do you never write?'

The girls did not get Henry to themselves again during his visit, and he still talked with reserve to them before their uncle and aunt. Their shyness had melted however and they teased him and joked with him so freely that Mrs Young sometimes fancied they were going too far. Laura had a curious conversation with her after Henry had gone. Her aunt fidgeted with her bracelets a little before she spoke. Then she observed, 'Henry seems to admire Nell.'

'Oh yes, he told me so,' Laura answered.

Mrs Young pondered. 'Do you know what Nell feels? I don't think your uncle would care for it; there is too great a difference in age.'

Laura suddenly saw the drift of her remarks and was so surprised that she could not find anything to say. She felt certain her aunt was mistaken; Henry belonged to her rather than to Nell. Yet the idea of marrying him had only just occurred to her; she was oddly surprised to find it had occurred at all. But later, very much later, when she was older and the gap between their ages mattered less, if Henry still wanted her she fancied she might marry him; her sister, she knew, would approve of it. She was positive that Nell had no ideas for herself about him, and she wondered how Nell would take their aunt's suggestion.

An hour later Nell came fuming into their sitting room.

'Lolly, did you hear what Aunt Carrie has been thinking?'

'About you and Henry?'

'Yes; did you ever hear anything so ridiculous? Of course she means it all for the best, but my dear Lolly – Henry! Did you feel how the springs groaned when he tried to get into our cart? I thought the poor ponies would turn round to protest.'

'I like his being tall,' said Laura defensively. 'When I am with him I feel safe.'

'Well, please do tell Aunt Carrie she need have no fears. As far as I am concerned the notion is preposterous. I shall be really rude if she says anything about it again.'

CHAPTER X

AFTER Henry left Laura felt restless and unoccupied. She did not want to paint but had nothing else to do. Margaret, away on a visit, was bringing her friend back to stay with her; there was no chance of Greek lessons for some time to come. The weather changed, turning oppressive and uncertain; for three nights they were kept awake by thunderstorms. Mrs Young was nervous and thought her heart had been affected; Birdie suffered from continual headaches.

Birdie's headaches disturbed the girls; they drove her more often into their sitting room. Though her right to it was now definitely limited she still retained a certain proprietory interest, partly because a corner cupboard was kept for medicines, partly because the room was so much cooler than her own that the girls had offered her the use of it whenever they were out. Birdie's and Laura's rooms both faced the drive, Birdie's window being almost over the porch. The trees on the other side of the gravel made them stuffy and the kitchen chimney came up the wall between the rooms. Laura's bedroom had two windows and she slept with her door open at night. Birdie's smaller room opened on the backstairs and if she left her door ajar the servants would be able to look in. To the girls this difficulty did not seem unsurmountable; a screen inside could ensure privacy. But Birdie had no screen.

'Well, Uncle would get one.'

'I beg you will say nothing to your uncle, either of you.'

Laura remembered a screen in the box room and a housemaid with some difficulty got it down for her. When it was dusted it looked quite presentable but Birdie was not particularly grateful. 'It is nice of you to think of me, Laura, but I don't want that great thing in my crowded little room.' So the screen went upstairs again but the weather remained thundery, and the next afternoon when the girls came back from their drive Birdie started up from a chair as they opened the door of the sitting room and snatched up a basin and a handkerchief. She had evidently been lying back with eau de cologne on her forehead, and the girls hardly knew which they resented more, her persistence in staying so long or her meekness in going away. She was wearing bedroom slippers and she failed to fasten the door; they listened with impatience to her shuffling retreat.

Nell flung up the window. 'D'you think we looked too furious?'

'I don't know. She always goes unless we tell her to stay.'

The next day Nell rode over to see the Hawleys. Mrs Young after lunch had decided it was too hot for driving and settled herself in an easy-chair for an afternoon's nap. Laura sat with her till she dozed off, then got up to leave the room. Her aunt immediately opened her eyes.

'What are you going to do till tea time, my dear?'

'I am not quite sure, Aunt Carrie. I must write some letters, I think.'

'I shall be so glad if you will write a little note for me. Sit at my escritoire and I will tell you what to say when you are ready.'

'I thought perhaps I would change first into a cooler dress.'

'Certainly, my dear; I am not in any hurry. Indeed I could quite well send a boy with the message.'

Laura escaped and went up to the sitting room. Birdie was lying on the sofa with closed eyes.

'Is that you, Laura?' she murmured. 'I am so sorry. I thought you would be driving with your aunt this afternoon.'

'Never mind; I've only come for a moment,' said Laura coldly. She collected her writing things without another word and stalked out, wondering where she could find solitude.

Her bedroom and her painting room would be too hot; if she went downstairs again Aunt Carrie would be sure to call her; Nell's cool bedroom seemed her only refuge. She could sit there undisturbed till it was nearly tea time; if Aunt Carrie wanted a note sent then there would still be time to scribble it. She pulled up a chair to the window, put the ink on the dressing table, and contented if not comfortable wrote several sheets to Margaret. At last she heard the sitting-room door open and a moment later Birdie looked reproachfully in. She did not go away but stood on the threshold, a grotesque apparition making an inarticulate appeal. In one hand she held a bowl with the eau de cologne bottle standing in it, a damp towel hung over her arm. She had evidently taken off her bodice for comfort, a limp cotton peignoir clung to her shoulders. Her face was yellow with red-stained eye sockets, her hair straggled to one side, her cap hung askew. Laura looked at her with distaste; she felt no pity. Such ugliness, such decay, ought not to walk abroad.

'Laura, why didn't you tell me you wanted to write upstairs?'

'I didn't mind where I wrote as long as I was alone.'

All her impatience sounded in her voice. Birdie's pleading brows straightened, her light eyes grew stony. With a fierce look on her pale little face she turned away. Laura was almost glad to have made her angry; she could face anger better than plaintiveness. When Birdie was plaintive Laura's conscience took her part, reminding her of the governess's homelessness. Enmity between them freed them both; Laura gave up her efforts to be kind and relapsed into a natural indifference; Birdie indulged her spite in petty reprisals. When once she felt she had settled the scores she became friendly again.

For some time after this she avoided Laura. She sat in her room in the afternoons with the door tight shut. And when the day came next for doing the flowers neither girl was called in to help.

Birdie did the flowers on Tuesdays and Saturdays. These were days of great importance to her. By ten o'clock she was waiting aproned in a little room near the garden door, a cupboard of a room fitted with shelves, a basin and a tap. Here she assembled her collection for filling; she seldom made changes in the array. Three squat vases came from the drawing room; these were milky grey-blue glass with frills round the rims. The study provided a silver container for one choice blossom; another was needed for the bracket by Mrs Young's chair. The hall had a huge glass trumpet fitting into a silver stand, which was useful for arum lilies and other tall flowers but tiresome to fill because the stand was heavy to carry and the glass holder would not keep upright by itself. To the dining room Birdie allowed a little variety; she waited to see what the gardener brought before she chose her vases. He would come with a basket of neatly cut bunches and sometimes a barrowful of flowering plants and ferns. With a couple of pots in his arms he might tiptoe behind her into the drawing room and discuss the arranging of the gilt jardinière. In the hall a tall palm stood in a cluster of smaller ones, and he always took a look at these before he went away. Laura liked the mornings best when the ferns were changed: for a time they gave the hall and passages a sweet earthy smell.

On her good days Birdie would ask the girls to help her with the vases, and then the confusion in the flower room lasted twice as long. Laura and Nell were more fastidious in their arrangements; and often ran out to catch the gardener and demand other colours or more of one sort. Birdie would grow impatient before they finished; doing the flowers was her duty, not theirs.

At present, to show her displeasure, she arranged the flowers alone; neither Laura nor Nell was allowed to help. In further protest she got out a vase that they both disliked and used it for the centre of the dining-room table. It was an elaborate affair of twisted silver branches springing from a base on a circular looking-glass tray. Each arm had a narrow mouth for holding flowers, and into each Birdie stuck a rose and a piece of maidenhair fern. She liked the vase because it saved her trouble: there were many arms but none would hold more than a couple of stalks. Laura grimaced when she sat down to dinner and saw the circling branches and meagre sprays. But the looking glass base began to please her, and she studied the reflections as the meal went on. Conversation flagged. The evening was extraordinarily oppressive, a heavy thunder haze cut off the light. Mrs Young finally ordered candles and when these were brought Laura lost all knowledge of what was going on. In an ecstasy she watched the open windows reflected as deep blue curves in the bowls of the tablespoons, and the warm flood of candlelight upon the level cloth. The looking-glass lake in the shadow of its sprays had become deep and remote, like water under trees. Its elaborate silver edge shone faintly blue in the twilight still. Then Mrs Young, who was growing nervous, signalled to a maid to close the shutters. Somebody passed behind Laura and cut off the evening light.

'What is the matter, my dear?' asked her uncle as Laura sighed.

'It looked so pretty with the windows open.'

'My dear, it is time to close them.' Her aunt spoke with irritation and her uncle went on with the story he was telling. He addressed himself however more particularly to Nell and Laura knew he was rebuking her for her lack of attention.

The storm that night broke the bad weather; when they woke next morning the air was clear and fresh. And with the morning came a letter from Margaret; she was back at The Shrubbery and longing to see Laura. She invited her to a picnic tea.

'Chloe is staying here,' ran the letter. 'I could not believe she was coming till we were in the train together; she is too fond of changing her mind. Unfortunately Father has changed his about going away. He does not leave till the end of the week and in the meanwhile he is unjust to Chloe. If you come and agree with me in admiring her qualities perhaps he will see there is more in her than he thinks. The trouble really is that he doesn't care for visitors. He says the house is already too full of his family. That is true, but I didn't mean to make him uncomfortable. He did say positively that he meant to go away today.'

So Margaret also had family difficulties. The thought gave Laura a certain consolation. But she could not fancy Mr Fraser hard to manage: Margaret must be clumsy in her approach to him. 'She admires too easily,' thought Laura in some disdain. Yet the recollection of Margaret's admiration for herself made her change for the picnic with special care; she chose a favourite mauve cotton dress that had shrunk in the wash. She had to lace a little tighter in order to wear it and adjusted the pad under the small bustle with some pride in her slimness. The dress was really too grand for a picnic, she thought; but it was old and the sleeves were beginning to wear out.

Mrs Young and Nell had ordered the carriage and dropped her early at the Frasers' gate. Nobody noticed her as she came up the drive; nobody seemed to be about when she walked in. But hearing voices from the library she peeped round the door and found Mr and Mrs Fraser sitting alone. They looked so contented together that she did not like to disturb them and was just going away again when he turned his head. 'Is that you, Laura? Come here and show yourself. We haven't seen you for a long time.'

He did not get up as she approached but held out his hand and took hers and kept it, running his thumb gently over her fingers as if he liked the feel.

'And where are you going so fine today, my Laura?'

'I'm going for a picnic with Margaret.'

'A picnic, my dear Laura, how can you be so rash? Six drops of rain will melt you like a sugar plum, a puff of wind will blow you off like thistledown, and a good hot sun will burn you brown. I can't risk letting you go for a picnic today.'

'You mustn't mind his teasing,' said his wife.

'She doesn't mind my teasing. She likes it; don't you, Laura? What a blessing it is there are girls left who can blush.'

'Oh please,' cried Laura, embarrassed but laughing, 'can you tell me if Margaret is waiting?'

'I've no idea what Margaret is doing. I expect she's still upstairs talking to that precious friend of hers.'

Laura again tried to take her hand away, but he held it tightly and glared at her under his shaggy brows.

'Child, have you heard of the emancipation of women?'

'Oh yes, I think so,' she said uncertainly.

'Well, some women ruin their own cause.'

'The door behind you is open,' interposed his wife.

'God bless my soul, my dear, the girl must know what I think of her unless she is a fool, which I don't take her to be. And Margaret shall know what I think before I leave. Heaven send my daughter a little more sense.'

Laura looked at Esther for amplification.

'My husband doesn't care for Margaret's friend, Miss Baldwin. I don't think she is as bad as he makes out. She is good to the children, they are enchanted with her, but she grows truculent with anyone who she thinks disapproves of her ways.'

Voices sounded in the hall and he let Laura go. 'Shut the door behind you,' he commanded, 'and don't let anybody into the room.'

The porch seemed to be crowded with people. The children had joined the expedition, an attention they did not often pay to their sister's friends. The newcomer was taller than Margaret, a striking figure in a dress of terra-cotta red crowned with an enormous peasant's hat. Her face was like a peasant's, brown with strong features and thickly marked eyebrows, and the hand she held out was square and firm. As she was introduced her eyes sought Laura's perhaps too boldly, but Laura would not return the glance. 'I don't like her; she is forward,' she told herself, and the next moment the impression was confirmed. As they collected their picnic baskets and debouched on the drive, James, Rob and Katy scampering ahead, the stranger turned an impudent face and said coolly: 'Tell me, weren't you being warned against me?'

Laura was for a moment too shocked to reply. That Margaret's guest should speak so of Margaret's father, a kind old man and Laura's particular friend, seemed to her almost horrible. Yet under her disapproval stirred a faint excitement. Such callousness reminded her of the days when she and Nell had revenged themselves on Birdie by saying wicked things about her under their breath. Loyalty to Mr Fraser drowned the unworthy pleasure. She looked coldly at the girl and said, 'Yes, I was.'

Chloe Baldwin showed no shame. The answer seemed to please her. She stared with such amusement that Laura realized she was being teased: the abrupt question had been put to see what she would say. She turned away to mark disapproval and at once Chloe began to race with the children. The basket she was carrying was big and heavy; she put it on her shoulder and ran sure-footed, her sandals treading easily on the tussocky grass. She caught little Kate and put her hat on her; the child looked like a mushroom under the huge brim. They turned back together laughing and Laura felt a pang of envy. She would have liked to run as fast as that, to have short curly hair cropped like a boy's, to wear sleeves that slipped back easily from the wrist, to rub a forehead with unconcern along a cool arm. This girl had free and easy manners, but there was something attractive about her all the same.

Nothing of this showed in Laura's voice as she turned to ask Margaret, 'Did she have her hair cut off because of illness?'

'Yes, but that was long ago. She likes it short. I hope you won't think Chloe too eccentric, Laura.'

'Oh, the heat!' cried Chloe, as they came up to her. 'How delicious it will be to bathe.'

'Bathe?' said Laura, surprised, and then she saw that James was carrying a bundle of towels.

'Father has made us a pool in the river. He rents two fields for the fishing, you know; but he never catches anything and so now he has had the weeds cleared away and a load of gravel put down. The boys have learned to swim quite well and Katy is getting on.'

They had crossed the road as Margaret was talking and made their way slowly down the hill to the stream. The Frasers' bathing place was half-way between the mill and the village, well sheltered by a steep slope on one side of the river and by a line of alders on the opposite bank. At the water's edge they were completely private and here the boys put down the bathing things.

'We'd better let them go in first,' said Margaret. 'If they bathe with us they only play tricks and stir up the water till it gets muddy.'

But the boys did not want to swim. They were building a harbour further downstream and they ran off at once to play there. Only Katy, Chloe's warmest admirer, stayed to be with her.

'I've brought Esther's bathing dress for you,' said Margaret to Laura. 'Do come in with us. It's not really muddy. If you go down by the steps you stand on gravel.'

But Laura shook her head in great embarrassment. Except for a couple of willows a few yards away there was no shelter anywhere for undressing and she felt far too shy to wrestle with her stays in the open. Margaret and Chloe were not so encumbered. 'I really would much rather not,' she said at last.

Margaret seemed disappointed and Chloe looked at her keenly. 'She doesn't know how we manage to undress,' she said. 'When we're ready perhaps she'll try.'

Margaret took her little sister off to the cover of the willows and Laura sat down unhappily on the bank. Chloe was undressing close beside her and Laura did not like to turn her head. But Chloe began to whistle so cheerfully that at last Laura thought she might venture a glance. She was curious to see what underclothes Chloe wore; Nell, when she heard the tale, would certainly want to know. As she had fancied, Chloe had no stays, her drawers were buttoned to a shaped bodice. She was undressing in perfect unconcern; as Laura looked she stepped out of her drawers and stood up in a straight chemise. Then she pulled on the legs of her bathing dress and worked it up under the chemise. She lifted an arm to wriggle her shoulders free and the stretched armpit showed a patch of strong black hair. Laura stared, horrified and yet queerly fascinated. The hair looked vigorous, the flesh white and firm. Both she and Nell were almost smooth and they thought only servants and old people had such mats of hair. The next minute Chloe caught her eye and Laura jerked her head away from the scrutinising gleam. This girl, she felt, was too quick at guessing thoughts.

And now Chloe stood on the bank fastening the buttons of her bathing dress. It was made of red serge, faintly nautical since it had a large collar trimmed with anchors in white braid. And it had short puffed sleeves and was worn without a skirt. The folds, purposely baggy, were held by a belt at the waist, the full trousers ended in bands below the knee.

Margaret came up in a similar dress of blue and Katy with her, a delightful naked figure. 'I hope you don't mind. She hasn't got a bathing dress,' her sister apologized to Laura.

'She can't mind unless she's inhuman,' broke out Chloe. 'Come, Kit, I'll catch you if you jump from the top step.'

She plunged in, her bathing dress swelling for an instant round her, then darkening and clinging as the water ran up it. Katy, squealing with delight on the steps, jumped and was caught in Chloe's strong arms. The two older girls played with her till she had had enough, and then Margaret took her away to dry. Before long Chloe came out of the water too and lay on the grass where the bank shelved less steeply and made a shallow beach. She turned her head and called to Laura who was sitting higher up, 'Take off your shoes and stockings and paddle here. There is gravel here and it won't hurt your feet.'

Laura was feeling so cut off from their fun that she obeyed at once. The cold water rippled pleasantly over her feet; Chloe watched with half-shut eyes as she lifted her skirts and went deeper in. At last she came back and sat down shyly by Chloe on the bank.

'I'm so glad I made you do that,' murmured Chloe. 'Has anyone told you you have pretty feet?'

Laura blushed, but she was saved from a reply by an onrush of the boys who came up in great hunger demanding tea. Margaret told Chloe to dress while the rest unpacked the picnic, and then they settled themselves comfortably in the shade of the willows. One of the baskets was full of bottles – a medicine bottle of weak tea for each of them, and for Laura the privilege of a cup as well. Margaret dealt out the provisions with a firm hand, and when all the children were seated Chloe came up. She refused offers of various comfortable places and sat down deliberately by Laura's side. And Laura suddenly felt weak and helpless, tired almost to the verge of tears. She felt that Chloe could do anything she liked with her, could please her by attracting or pain by shocking her. And she was helpless because she did not want to escape, though she could not tell yet whether she liked or hated this strange girl. A keen delight shot through her as Chloe sat down, equally keenly she wanted to get up and run away.

As if she had read Laura's mind, Chloe was very gentle. She sat without talking, seemingly lost in thought. But if Laura wanted anything Chloe found it for her; she waited on her quietly, Laura hardly felt her move. Margaret was busy attending to the children; the young Frasers were much too hungry to look after their guests. And so Laura and Chloe found themselves allies, understanding each other's needs in a surrounding indifference.

When the first edge had been taken off their appetites the children drank out of their bottles and began to talk. Robert, who was sitting opposite the visitors and had stared at them unwinkingly for a long time, put down his bottle at last and observed with great solemnity, 'Your dresses don't look very nice together.'

'Don't you think so, Robbie? Terra cotta and mauve? Well, I wanted to sit beside Miss Young to show her that my heart is of gold though my manners are bold.'

'Oh, that's a rhyme.'

'It is. I made it on purpose.'

'She's very clever,' he remarked, conversationally.

James now directed his attention to Laura.

'Why do you have a cup when you drink?'

'I'm afraid I might spill my tea if I drank out of a bottle. And I'm so thirsty I don't want to waste a drop.'

'She must drink out of her bottle,' shouted Katy, who was excited. 'Chloe, Chloe, you tell her not to use her cup.'

'Oh, I'm going to think out much worse things for her to do,' said Chloe.

'What? What?' cried the child, but Rob said stoutly, 'I shan't let you. Laura's nice.'

'So she is. Then perhaps I won't tease her after all.' Chloe gave Laura a quick sidelong smile. Laura smiled back; she was no longer afraid. She leant against the willow trunk feeling absurdly happy. The sweet tepid tea, the sun on her bare feet, the bathing dresses and towels scattered over the hot bank, the tiny murmur of the stream behind her, and Chloe at her side, enigmatic and strange but protective as a hill, all these things filled her with a measureless content. Happiness stretched before her like an unbroken plain. She had travelled a long way since the morning.

Margaret had lost the ribbon from her hat. 'I'll make a trimming for it,' said Chloe idly. She reached up and stripped a few twigs from the willow and twisted them into a neat hoop. The result was not extravagant and Margaret looked absurdly pleased when she put her hat on. As they wandered home through the fields nearer the road Chloe picked some scabious and made another wreath.

'This is for you,' she said to Laura, but Laura shook her head. She did not want to copy Margaret and she found an easy excuse.

'My aunt and my sister may drive past us on the road. I don't know what they would think if they saw me wearing a wreath.'

'Will you object if I put it on?'

'Oh, not at all. I am sure it will be becoming.'

'I see, I see,' said Chloe, teasingly. 'The stranger may look mad but not the daughter of the Big House.'

As it happened the mauve went well with the terra cotta. In her straight tunic with the flowers in her hair she looked almost Grecian; like a wood nymph, Margaret said.

Laura had been joking when she spoke of the carriage, but they had hardly left the fields for the road before she heard horses behind them and became uncomfortably aware that they made a queer procession. Margaret, green garlanded, was carrying bathing dresses, Katy was dancing about in Chloe's huge hat, Chloe in any place would attract attention, and the little boys, untidy and dirty, trailed immense willow wands. She quickened her pace, for the Shrubbery gate was close by and she hoped they might reach the drive before they were overtaken. But at the top of the hill the horses began to trot, Margaret stopped to call the children off the road, Chloe turned and stared into the carriage, and Laura looked round to see a horrified recognition creep into the eyes of aunt and sister. The coachman, not noticing her, drove steadily on; the ladies were too surprised to call out. Aunt Carrie's flowered bonnet trembled towards Nell in an agitated enquiry as the brougham turned the corner in a cloud of dust.

'Oh dear, I'm afraid we looked very untidy,' faltered Margaret.

'Is that your sister?' asked Chloe. 'How lovely she is, like a china ornament. No wonder she was shocked at seeing us.'

The little boys, who had run ahead to swing on the gate, suddenly began to shout and wave their arms. 'They're waiting for you,' they hallooed to Laura, and she saw that the carriage had stopped after all and was drawn up a little farther down the road.

'Come and say how do you do,' she begged her friends uneasily, but Margaret hesitated and Chloe spoke for both.

'We are much too untidy and dirty, Laura dear. If you apologize and explain that we are ashamed perhaps your aunt will think better of us. Mayn't Margaret bring me one day to call? I should like to see your portrait of her.'

'Oh yes; do come. Come tomorrow.' Laura could wait no longer. With a hasty goodbye she ran away.

CHAPTER XI

THE carriage door shut like the door of a prison. Laura's hour of liberty was over. Now she had to account for her actions to her gaolers and there were clearly two gaolers, not one. Nell's eyes turned to her sister coldly, took in every detail of her disarray. Aunt Carrie was at present more inquisitive than shocked; the surprise had left her animated.

'Laura, my dear, how untidy you look. But I must say you are no worse than any of your party. I have never seen people in such a state. Were those two dirty boys the little Frasers? Where had they been to get so muddy?'

'They had been playing by the river. We went down there for a picnic, you know.'

'A picnic? There were tea things in those baskets? But were the flies bad where you were sitting? Why had Margaret leaves round her hat?'

'Oh, Aunt Carrie, it was just a joke. She lost the proper trimming so we made her a wreath.'

'I see. It certainly looked very strange. And the dark girl, who was she? I did not care for her appearance at all. I suppose Margaret met her at College.'

Laura said nothing and her aunt went on, 'And why were you carrying so many wet towels? Had one of the children fallen in?'

It was impossible to evade the questions. Aunt Carrie's curiosity was thoroughly aroused.

'They had been bathing,' said Laura with some hesitation.

'Bathing in the river?' Mrs Young was horrified.

'Mr Fraser wants the boys to swim, so he has made them a

nice bathing pool with gravel at the bottom.'

'Where is it?'

'In the low meadows.'

'So close to the village. I have never heard of such a thing.'

'It's quite sheltered. No one could see us.'

The choice of the pronoun startled Mrs Young. 'Laura, I trust you didn't go in.'

'Oh no, Aunt Carrie.'

'Did Margaret, then?'

Laura tried to sound unconcerned. 'She often does.'

'I cannot understand Mr Fraser's allowing it. I wonder no one in the village has complained. Your uncle would not care for such behaviour at all. He can have no idea what has been going on.'

Mrs Young fell into a disapproving silence and Laura tried to signal to Nell. But Nell kept her face turned obstinately away; her profile was expressionless. Laura felt piqued: it was not Nell's business to disapprove of her sister's escapades. 'I don't see why you should be cross,' she ventured as they went upstairs together when the drive was over. 'Bathing in the river isn't a crime.'

'Oh, I don't mind about the bathing in the river. If you like mud, by all means swim in it. But I do think, Lolly, you might look tidy afterwards.' Nell's voice quivered with scorn as she stood at the door of her room. 'If you could have seen yourself when we met you on the road. It's all very well to have friends like the Frasers, who do unconventional things, but when it comes to walking about with them draggle-tailed near the village, in a sort of dirty procession that looks quite mad – that awful girl with flowers in her hair, and all those damp towels – I don't see why I shouldn't be cross. Even with Aunt Carrie I felt quite degraded. Suppose I had been with the Hawleys, what could I have said to them?'

Laura was so hurt that she walked straight into her bedroom and locked herself in. All her energies for a moment went into not crying. She seemed to be pushing a door in her mind against an intruding pain. Presently the pain attacked less fiercely and she was able to relax her pressure against it. She could now spare time for her appearance; she went to the glass and stared at a sunburnt face and rough hair. Certainly she was looking a little wild. And when she turned up the hem of her dress she found what Nell had noticed: several inches at the back were stained with mud where she had let her skirts drag when she was paddling. She was too old, she supposed, for such adventures; Nell was right to fear what people might think.

Yet, and here Laura plumped down on a chair and stared at the carpet, yet she could not feel entirely ashamed of herself. She was sorry she had been caught looking dirty and untidy; but dirt and untidiness were little to pay for such an afternoon. Her mind glowed as sometimes her body glowed after hard riding; she felt she had used powers not needed in her daily life, had branched out like a tree with new space to grow in. But it would be difficult to explain all this to Nell, almost impossible to define the source of the enjoyment. The sun, the river, the children, the messy scrambling picnic – nothing remarkable in any of these. Nell would enjoy the bathing story when she had climbed down from her present mood, but even the bathing could not quite account for Lolly's rapture. It was plain that the presence of Chloe had brought the keenest pleasure – 'And oh, my poor Lolly, there you go again,' Laura scolded herself aloud in her sister's voice. For there was no doubt about it: she was at the beginning of a 'craze', one of these enthusiasms Nell so much deplored.

Though it was not exactly a craze, she reflected, taking off her shoes, it was something nearer a trial of strength. She unhooked her dress and got out of it, then let down her hair, trying all the time to think out what she felt.

'You see,' she told an invisible listener by the washstand, 'I like people to be cleverer than I am, so that my brain can pull against theirs. That's why I like Margaret; and though I don't know how clever Chloe is I shall enjoy hearing what she thinks about my pictures. I suppose I could have a craze for a stupid person but I should be ashamed of myself if I did.

'And then the person must be stronger than I am, so that the tug of war is not one-sided. It's not quite even between me and Margaret. I have discovered that she minds too much what I think of her, so I can't like her as much as I did. I suppose if she were the stronger she would stop liking me.'

She had almost finished dressing before she decided that a craze most easily developed into a friendship if the other person's upbringing and manners resembled her own. And for this reason she thought rather guiltily of Chloe, for Chloe's manners embarrassed her slightly and would always make a friendship difficult, since her family would dislike them far more than she.

Arguing the matter out made her feel much happier, but Nell when they met again was inclined to be stiff and Mrs Young was wrapped in a querulous disapproval. 'There will soon be no one left for me to talk to,' thought Laura, looking at them both and remembering that she was still on bad terms with Birdie; and she took her place at dinner in a defiant mood. She guessed from her uncle's manner that he had heard about the bathing, but he was too full of other news to remain serious long.

'The carriage is coming tomorrow,' he told them all. 'I heard definitely from London this evening. It will come by train; I think I shall go to watch the unloading and then drive back in the afternoon. What are the plans for tomorrow, my dear?'

'The Hawleys are coming to tea. Lady Hawley is bringing her sister.'

'Ah, that's a pity. I cannot take you for a drive. Well, I daresay a detail or two may need adjusting. You must all come out with me the following day.'

He was elated as a boy before a treat. After dinner he kept them all up late demanding his favourite songs from Nell. Nell trilled, Laura did her best with the accompaniments, good-will seemed restored before they went to bed. But the sisters kissed each other goodnight without mentioning the afternoon: Laura's faults, Nell's rudeness, had not been forgiven.

The next day was one of great anticipation. Even Mrs Young went round to the stables to see what arrangements had been made for the new carriage. Laura and Nell went with her, but as soon as she could Laura left the others and went back to the house. She had anticipations of her own.

She was convinced that her friends would call and she meant to put the box room straight before they came. She worked hard till eleven but no one arrived. Then as she looked at her canvases leaning against the walls she suddenly grew dissatisfied with the crosslights in the room. The attic was good for painting, but it made a bad gallery. She wondered if she dared take some of the pictures downstairs.

She went down to look. The sitting room was empty; Birdie was doing flowers and Nell still out of doors. The big north window gave just the light she wanted; she decided to move her best pictures down. She grew so absorbed arranging them that the morning flew by and she had no idea of the time when Nell came in.

'Indeed,' Nell said, 'this is a new departure. I thought this was my music room, not your studio.'

'Don't you think they look rather nice here?' Laura suggested. 'Let's pretend I'm showing and you've come to buy.'

Nell hooked her arm round her sister's neck and they made the round of the gallery. Nell was a critic on the conservative side. The only picture she couldn't bear was the one of Margaret. 'It just shows me what an unselfish person she must be. For if you made me look like that, however artistic you were, I simply should never speak to you again.' She was in high good humour, but Laura wondered uncomfortably what she would say if she knew why the pictures had been set out.

Laura grew more uneasy as the day went on. Mr Young drove off to the station in triumph after lunch; the girls waving him a fervent goodbye from the porch. Laura felt he would like them both to be there to celebrate his return, but she slipped off none the less in great haste to The Shrubbery. She felt she was silly to go: she risked disappointing her uncle, and Margaret and Chloe might not be meaning to call. She told herself she was going to prevent their coming, that Nell would never forgive her if they arrived while the Hawleys were there. But a wish to see Chloe, strong yet unacknowledged, made her feel self-conscious about going at all and the expedition became a guilty one.

It was also useless. Nobody seemed to be at home. After searching through the empty rooms Laura tried the kitchen and here she found Bessy asleep in a chair, her apron thrown over her head to keep off the flies. The girl woke up as Laura came in and showed a flushed face stupid with sleep. Then she started up, bewildered and ashamed, with bungling accounts of just having dropped off and earnest protestations that Miss Laura should never catch her again. It was some time before Laura had a chance to speak; she was not sure in the end that the girl understood the message. Bessy however promised to remember and Laura, very cross and hot, hurried away fretting because she had made herself late.

She was asked for. The new carriage had come and the Hawleys, arrived early, were in the drawing room. She flung off her hat and ran downstairs.

Lady Hawley had brought over a large feminine party, conversation was in full swing, and Birdie was just ready to pour out. Rose and Nell were talking to the easiest of the visitors, a cheerful widow willing to be amused. Laura found a place near the principal guests and quickly wished herself away. 'This is the artist,' said Lady Hawley to her sister and a formidable Miss Forncett turned a long gaze on Laura. Her deep fringe and mauve dress suggested aestheticism, though modulated not to shock the circle she was in. She was tall and fair and fragile-looking, but a certain air of conceit, perhaps the very graciousness with which she turned, annoyed Laura who was still feeling hot after her walk.

'You paint?' Intensity sounded in the murmured words.

'Only a little.'

Miss Forncett smiled as if she knew better, but Laura was

saved from more questions by the entry of Mr Young. He came from the stables where he had been superintending the putting up of the carriage. Lady Hawley asked questions, her husband would be eager to know all about it. He promised her a visit of inspection after tea.

'Well, what d'you think of it, Lolly?' He came over presently when he had finished chatting to the others.

'Uncle, I haven't seen it; I was too late,'

'Late?'

'I went for a walk after lunch.'

He turned away and Laura felt overwhelmed with shame. He thought she took no interest in a matter affecting him keenly. She longed to explain that it was not lack of interest but the complexity of her own affairs that kept her away from the stables. Yet, if she had dared to explain, her excuses would sound trivial. In fussing over a visit from a friend she had ignored the triumphant issue of six months' negotiations. She sat in deep dejection holding an empty cup. The talk rippled on without a word from her.

Suddenly Lady Hawley addressed her again. 'My sister is hoping to see some of your pictures, Laura. We have been telling her about them and she is so much interested.'

'I described them as well as I could,' called Rose. 'Nell has taken me up to your painting room, you know.'

'You have a studio?' enquired Miss Forncett. 'Ah, what a lucky girl.'

'It's only a box room,' explained Laura quickly. 'Right up at the top of the house.'

'You mustn't dream of going up there, Miss Forncett. Laura, couldn't you bring some of your pictures down?'

'Oh Aunt Carrie, I have so little.'

'We musn't tease her. I know how hard it is to show one's efforts.' Miss Forncett's tone was provocative, but Laura sat mute.

'Why,' shrilled Birdie from behind the urn, 'there are half a dozen on show in the sitting room now.'

The malice in her voice made an instant's awkwardness.

Then Rose good-naturedly jumped up and turned to Nell. 'Come along, we'll fetch one or two down. Laura is too modest about what she does.'

'I'll come too. They may be wet,' said Laura, getting up quickly. As she left the room she heard amusement at her haste. She stalked upstairs behind the others in her ugliest mood. She would pick out all her most uncompromising studies. The drawing room was insistent and should be shocked.

But when she saw her patient canvases, not pictures but individuals, so far detached from her that each had personality, so much a part of her that she saw herself in each, she could not bear to let them go where they might be laughed at. She only chose some quiet landscapes and a portrait of Nell that her uncle liked.

But Rose snatched up the biggest picture. 'I must take this, Laura. I know you'll be angry. But I want to watch Aunt Lillian's face when she looks at it.'

'Not that one, please.'

'Oh Lolly, don't be serious.' The girls ran off giggling with their spoils.

'Ah, now we shall see,' said Mr Young urbanely as the procession re-entered the drawing room. He was standing on the hearth rug, a picture of studied confidence, but Laura felt his underlying nervousness. His difficult niece was at present on trial, he was not certain what part he had to play. Aunt Carrie sat up on the sofa in vague alarm and Birdie craned like a vulture over the tea table. They were all watching to see how she behaved.

Laura propped up two pictures on the grand piano; Miss Forncett lifted glasses and trailed across the room. 'Ah,' she breathed out slowly, looking for one to the other. 'Charming, charming. Yes, I see.'

'She's a silly woman,' thought Laura suddenly. 'She doesn't know whether she likes them or not.' And when the lorgnettes had finished their peering she changed the canvases in silent scorn. To Mr Young her silence seemed disappointment and since Miss Forncett had not yet said anything encouraging he came up to the piano in defence of his niece.

'Laura has suffered perhaps from having no master lately. You miss your painting lessons, don't you, my dear?'

The girl was dumb. Miss Forncett looked round for another picture and Mr Young went on with his difficult task.

'Let me take that big thing you are holding, Rose. Ah, this must be the famous portrait of Margaret. She is the daughter of the novelist, George Fraser. They are great friends of ours, and live close by. Miss Fraser kindly sat in the blazing sun for Laura with an old carriage umbrella over her head.'

Miss Forncett stared in a sort of horror and Mrs Young left the sofa and came across. 'My dear, what a dreadful picture,' she said simply, and Rose and Nell began to laugh at her unaffected dismay.

'But isn't it?' she demanded. 'It's not like Margaret. Laura, why did you give her a green face?'

'It looked like that with the light coming through the umbrella.'

'But Margaret's face could never be so green. She has a pretty complexion, I assure you, Miss Forncett.'

Her uncle looked at the work again and achieved a chuckle.

'It really was like that,' protested Laura.

'I have seen people very green,' said the good-natured widow.

'On a Channel crossing, perhaps,' laughed Lady Hawley. 'Well, what does Miss Forncett think?'

Miss Forncett turned to her host. 'I think Miss Young chooses an unbecoming light for her subjects. I can see that the face might be green, of course, but it is not pretty. I would rather have waited till the light was not so fierce.'

'But fierce light is so interesting,' broke in Laura.

'Ah, you beginners choose the hardest subjects.' Then seeing Laura redden Miss Forncett added gently, 'You musn't mind my little criticism, my dear. I am sure you had good reason for what you did.'

'I don't mind criticism,' said Laura at breaking point. 'But I do hate having to show my pictures.'

A high note in her voice made the guests uncomfortable. Lady Hawley picked up her gloves and made a move to go. What about the landau, she asked her host; might she go round the stables before driving home? Chairs were shifted, the guests trailed out and the three girls were left alone.

Rose had long since dropped the grand manner she had worn when they first met and she now rushed up to Laura crying, 'I am so sorry I brought down that picture. I never thought you would really mind. Of course Aunt Lillian wouldn't like it; I'm sure it's too modern for her. She paints such old-fashioned things, you know: moss roses and landscapes with a slope across the foreground. All her pictures have a slope in one corner; she never makes them flat in front as you do.'

Rose rattled on as Nell collected the canvases and Laura smiled and tried to still the shaking of her hands. Some calamity had taken place; she was not sure what, but Rose's kindness plainly showed there was some reason to be kind. Guiltily she remembered the scene in the drawing room; she had contrived to embarrass a roomful of guests. Events were moving too fast for her management; she could hardly recover from one scrape before she was in another. Suddenly very tired and listless she stacked the canvases to put them somewhere out of sight.

'We'll help you carry them.'

'Oh, please don't trouble.' Rose's sympathy was becoming oppressive.

'Well, you'd better take them away,' said Nell. 'You were a goose, Lolly, to leave them in the sitting room.'

In the end they carried the pictures to the top of the house, then trooped into Nell's bedroom that Rose might tidy herself. 'I ought to go down,' she said before the glass, patting her hair and tilting forward her pretty hat. 'Mother must have ordered the horses by now. I think I can hear her in the garden.'

Nell, lolling on the window seat, looked out across the lawn and her face puckered in dismay.

'Lolly, quick. Run down and catch them. Here's your precious friend Margaret coming with that extraordinary girl. They've just got into the garden now. For heaven's sake go and bring them in by the side door and keep them upstairs till everybody's gone. Uncle will be furious if he meets them and I'm sure I don't know what the others will think.'

'What girl?' cried Rose, popping out her head.

'Be careful; they'll see you. A most dreadful friend of Lolly's. She's wearing an aesthetic terra-cotta dress.'

Laura rushed down the backstairs and out into the shrubbery, guided by whispered directions from above. She heard Chloe's voice, then other voices, and arrived on the lawn a second too late. Lady Hawley, Miss Forncett and Mrs Young had just encountered Margaret and Chloe. All five were drawn up in a hostile group. Unexpected meetings alarmed Margaret; in her most bungling manner she now made the introductions, and Chloe, missing the muttered name, imagined she had met Mrs Young. Without a trace of the shyness afflicting Margaret she turned to Lady Hawley as if they knew each other and said, 'We have come to apologize for our appearance yesterday. I hope you were not too shocked to find your niece in such bedraggled company.'

Then seeing no understanding in the features confronting her she changed her tone and added more formally, 'Miss Young invited me to look at her pictures. I so much want to see the portrait of Margaret.'

Miss Forncett's nostrils twitched. She looked deeply offended. Lady Hawley said briefly, 'Miss Young is not my niece.'

Chloe's colour rose at the curtness of the tone and Laura hurried forward into the group. When they saw her the guests said cold goodbyes and moved off quickly with their host.

Margaret went crimson; Chloe turned to Laura. 'My dear,

what has happened? Have we come at an unfortunate time?'

'Oh,' cried Laura, 'it has been a dreadful afternoon. I left a message for you; didn't you get it?'

'Nothing to make sense. Bessy said you had come but she couldn't tell what you had wanted.'

'I wish I had written a note.'

'It's always safer.'

'Well, don't let's worry about that now. We're here at the wrong time so we'd better be off again quickly. But Laura,' cried Chloe, 'just tell us what has been happening. You look so miserable.'

Laura described the scene with Miss Forncett. Chloe listened with great indignation. 'And then I came and said you had promised to show me your pictures. Well,' she went on stoutly, 'I am glad I spoke so loud. She looks a tiresome woman who deserves to be put down. But Laura, Laura, you musn't mind so much.'

'I do, you know. She's tiresome, but I mind what she said about my paintings and I mind much more that I offended her.'

'Bless you, don't look so tragic. You musn't let them worry you. Stiff and ceremonious people like that! You're real, you know, they're half sham. If you don't mind them they can't hurt you.'

'Oh yes, they can.'

'Well, I suppose they can. But you must be strong enough to bear it, my dear.'

She had taken both Laura's hands and was peering into her face, her big features twisted in sympathy.

'Come up now to my painting room,' pleaded Laura. She wanted the protection of this warmth in the house.

Bur Chloe shook her head. 'It wouldn't be strategic. I still hear voices chattering somewhere. We'll go now; and if your uncle asks us why we didn't stay tell him we were much too frightened to come in. Then perhaps his heart will soften and you may ask us tomorrow instead.'

Margaret glanced to see if this boldness offended Laura, but in fact she was grateful for Chloe's plain speaking. She walked with them to the garden railings and watched till they climbed the stile and went into the wood.

The woods were at their most splendid in the blaze of evening sun; the pathway beyond the stile made a cave in a golden wall. In contrast to this glory the deserted garden looked cold, the shadow of house and trees creeping out across the lawn. Laura coming back again felt lonely and oppressed, and panic seized her as she turned into the shrubbery and saw her uncle waiting at the end of the walk.

CHAPTER XII

HE stood like a monument brooding over her approach. She felt rather than heard the words 'I want to speak to you,' and he led the way to his study in a terrifying silence.

The study windows faced the drive and the late sun through the trees dappled the screen in the fireplace and the littered mantelpiece. He went to his writing table and stood looking down; Laura sat timidly in the big armchair. She had hardly been inside the room since that afternoon in May when she had come to beg for her Greek lessons.

The ugly little study was unlike any other room in the house; even its smells were not to be met with elsewhere. From the gun rack by the door came the whiff of oil, but this faint breath vanished quickly in the richer flavour of leather from driving gloves on a shelf above the musty encyclopedias. Nearer the writing table a medicine cupboard was insistently pharmaceutical, the sharp smell of pig powders prevailing. And like some dark colour the background of the rest, the room was rich with scent of cigars.

Today Laura felt more keenly than ever the elusiveness of her uncle's nature. The study showed her an uncle she might have loved, a man who cherished the muddled room in the state he had always known it. But this man dimly guessed at was kept hidden from her, and the figure at the writing table was the uncle who was her guardian – cold, reserved, arrived too late in life at the fulfilment of boyhood wishes. In offending him she offended two people: the man proud of possession, the man loving his home. It was with this double anger that he faced her now.

'Laura, I must confess you are very much disappointing me. You are disappointing both your aunt and me. Here you are, settled in your new home with everything possible to make you happy: health, talents, possessions, and the affection of your sister, even if you do not value that of older people. You have liberty: we encourage your studies; you are seldom asked to do what is irksome to you. You have varied companionship, the choice unforced – for so far, though you know I prefer some of your friends to others, I have not asked you to forgo any. And in spite of all this, where you might lead an active and happy life you allow yourself to sink into your old moodiness, are self-centred, wrapped up in your personal occupations and inclined to show unfriendliness to those who criticize.'

Laura sat rigid, saying nothing.

'And that is not all. If you merely showed unfriendliness, behaved to everyone as you behaved in the drawing room today, though distressed I should consider that you were still uneducated, had not outgrown your earlier awkwardnesses. As a child, you remember, you were shy and diffident and when you first grew up I think you went out too little. I blame myself for not providing for you better, but while your grandfather was alive my position was difficult, and your aunt has never been strong enough for much entertaining. I had hoped that your fuller life here would soon bring you ease and that you would enjoy the gaieties we could not give you earlier.'

'I think I am unsociable,' ventured Laura.

'Perhaps. But I fancy the trouble comes less from dislike of society than from a determination to have friends of your own choosing. And, Laura, I do not care for the friends you choose. I notice in you as in many women a preference for odd and unusual acquaintances. To my mind there is something unpleasant in this preference and it disgusts me to see a niece of mine turning from friends of her own standing to vulgar intruders.'

'I could never bear vulgarity,' cried Laura hotly.

'Does it not offend you that a girl by her dress and her manner should almost call for attention to herself? That seems to me the truest vulgarity. I was distressed half an hour ago at the rudeness offered to Miss Forncett, but I was shocked to discover that Miss Baldwin came here by your invitation, that you were willing to accept her judgment where you showed openly you mistrusted ours. I was amazed to think her the sort of person you care for. Indeed Laura, it seems to me that unhealthy enthusiasms are leading you to accept what you would abhor in your right senses. I tell you plainly that I do not wish Miss Baldwin to come again and that I shall be glad if you can contrive to see less of Margaret Fraser. This absorption in friendship brings no good. The Greek lessons for the present must be given up; and you will please me better during the remainder of the summer if you will visit and drive more regularly with your aunt and try to overcome your unsociability.'

Laura had risen and stood facing him. Both were trembling, but he was the more composed. 'I am going out to dinner; I shall not see you again tonight. Think over what I have said and believe me, my dear: I am severe only for your ultimate good. Of all people who suffer from errors of judgment, women, I am positive, suffer most.'

He held the door for her and she went out: out of the room, out of the house, out of the garden. She did not know what she was doing till the clatter of pigeons' wings startled her and she found herself at the edge of the wood with the fourth door of the kitchen garden swinging open behind her. The place was uglier than it had been when she last came; nettles had grown up, tall and rank, and the inter-locked spruce boughs in the shadow of the wall made a mysterious twilight of their own. The coarse smell of the nettles filled her with disgust, but she thought she heard voices of people pursuing and she let the door slam and plunged into the wood, stamping through the nettles, pushing between branches, while the grey twigs caught at her hair and pulled it into wisps and more pigeons flapped in terror above her, feathers eddying where they had flown. At last she came to a clearing where a tree had fallen. Birds had nested above it at one end and the broken branches were whitened with droppings and stuck with down. Laura moved a yard or two away and then very tired stretched herself on the pine needles with her head on the trunk of the tree. She lay staring upward, at first afraid to think. The tops of the spruces were still living and green, and these, just yellowed by the last light of the sun, made a frame for a peaceful evening sky with small pink clouds in the blue. Sky and clouds looked unfriendly and remote; she seemed to lie at the bottom of a great grey well.

The quiet of this shadowy place at last melted her terror. But it brought no ease, for as her terror melted something ugly and hidden below began to rise to the surface. Presently she came upon the word "unhealthy". It was this that floated in her consciousness, this above all that made her afraid. Her thoughts shrank from it as from an evil thing and yet were constantly drawn back to poke and peer. And by degrees by touching they grew familiar with it and with familiarity the infection spread. Her uncle, she began to feel, had used the word deliberately, hinting at something he was afraid to speak. He had some ugliness lurking in his mind concerning her, and in anger meaning to wound her he had let it appear. There was a thin line of cruelty in her uncle, a suspicious cruelty born of lurking interest. Nobody knew of it, he was much too careful. Had she found him out because she was strange too? Was she in some way unlike other people? Nell laughed at her, Margaret called her odd.

She thought of things that had happened during her friendship with the Frasers, of the pang she felt when Robbie threw his arms round his mother, of Margaret looking hungrily for a kiss at the stile. Yet she could look back on these without disturbance; her greatest fault here she knew had been an impatient zeal. The Frasers stimulated her, she pursued them injudiciously; no wonder her family had grown alarmed. But there was more than this in her uncle's accusation: Laura lay still an instant, summoning up her courage. Then she forced herself to think of Chloe. The thought pierced like a sword and she writhed in self-loathing, a disgust so violent that it almost made her sick. In yesterday's pleasure there had been something shameful. Of her feeling for Chloe what her uncle said was true.

Immense exhaustion swept her. She might have lain there for hours if the outside bell, faintly clanging, had not told her the time. She shook the pine needles from her clothes, sped back in the dusk and was in and upstairs before anybody caught her. Birdie however met her at the bedroom door.

'Really , Laura, you try everybody's patience. Look at your hair, all ends – you will never be ready in time. Where have you been to get into such a state?'

Laura was late for dinner as Birdie prophesied and afterwards excused herself very early for bed. She heard Nell look in about an hour later but stayed buried in pillows and did not call out. She could not bear Nell near her at present; Nell must never know what her uncle had said.

Her sister moved to and fro in the room across the passage, the maids went heavy-footed up to bed. When these noises had died away Laura felt very lonely. She lay in the darkness fighting an invading disgust. It crept up through her thoughts like a stealthy enemy; she could beat it back but it forced her to keep on constant guard against its recurrence; the strain of her anxiety passed into her sleep. Suddenly she found herself staring up in terror. There was a ladder in her room and her uncle was climbing it. She could see his white face through the rungs, looking cruelly down. He was putting a poison on the canopy over her bed. It was a horrible poison, green like suppuration. Her eyes strained from their sockets, in her terror she could not move.

Then a thought struck her. She was not really unhealthy: the poison was heaped on the other side of the canopy, and if she willed hard enough she could stop its coming through. So she stared with all her might at the stretch of dry linen, willing the poison not to spread. But she was unhealthy, she was not truly healthy. A green stain began to mark the underside of the cloth. In spite of her agony it grew slowly darker, wet-looking. Presently it would drip.

The sharpness of her terror pierced the dream. She found herself awake, gasping in a violent sweat, her eyes fixed on the damask over her head where a trefoil was just visible in the uncertain light. For the rest of her life, she thought, she would hate that pattern; she flung herself over in bed to avoid seeing it. Everything outside the window was hushed and still; it would be a long time to morning yet.

She tried to think about her nightmare, but her thoughts would not meet it. They ran back from it, jostling like railway trucks on a siding. They had jostled one another disconnected like this on that last morning in Norwood when she had tried to look back on her dream about Nell. Some dreams were too terrible for the mind to bear.

And here she was lying, facing the window of that earlier nightmare. She wished she had not remembered this, for now she could not forget it. Nightmares come true when everything goes wrong. Everything had gone wrong for her lately. Could her dream be coming true? She dozed off to sleep again, feeling two deep wounds. One was disgust at the poison; it tingled like a burn. And fear for Nell's safety throbbed like a dull pain in her head.

She woke up pale and heavy, dressing slowly for breakfast. At the door of the dining room she met her uncle coming out. She shuddered, and then controlled herself enough to murmur good morning. He concealed impatience by looking bland.

'My dear, do you feel quite well?' said Mrs Young, when she saw her.

'I have rather a headache,' Laura confessed.

'You certainly don't look fit to go out driving today in the new carriage. What a pity!'

'Oh, Aunt Carrie, I don't want to miss my drive. If I take one of your cachous and lie down now I am sure I shall be all right by this afternoon.'

'Well, you had better go back to bed after breakfast. Ring

the bell and tell them to get your room ready now.'

Nell took her sister upstairs and helped her undress. Laura's head ached so much by now she could hardly stand.

'Nell, will you promise faithfully to wake me? I don't know what Uncle will think if I miss this drive.'

Nell hesitated. 'Listen, I'll tell you what I'll do. I'll look in before I go down to lunch and say "Lolly" quite loudly, and if you're nearly awake you'll probably hear me. But if you're still very fast asleep I'll leave you alone; it's bad to get up too soon if you've had a headache. I'll explain to Uncle; I'm sure he won't mind. We shall come back very cheerful at tea time. You'll be well again by then and everything will go right.'

'I hope it will. It's time it did,' murmured Laura from the bed.

'Did Uncle say something horrid last evening? I knew he had scolded you, I felt it in the air.'

'I won't tell you now.' Laura's voice quivered and Nell sat down on the edge of the bed.

'Lolly, it was very unkind of us to take those pictures. Rose is nice, you know, she was quite upset to find what she had done. She talked about it again when you had gone out of the room. And when she felt sorry I felt a thousand times worse, for I knew poor Lolly would mind and I took them just the same.'

Laura opened her eyes to smile at her sister, then shut them again with a little grimace.

'That's not crossness, only headache,' she managed to say.

'Poor little Lolly, I'll love you and leave you alone.' Nell kissed the tip of her nose, a mark of special tenderness, Laura nodded her head to show appreciation, heard the door close and fell asleep.

* * *

She woke a long time afterwards, knowing Nell had called her. She fancied she had stirred at once but her watch said a quarter past two; the carriage, she knew, had been ordered for half past. She raised herself on one elbow, feeling stupefied; her body moved but her brain seemed to be still asleep. When she got out of bed she was too dazed to be steady, she propped herself against a chair and put on some clothes. Her hair half done, she was wondering what to wear for the drive when she heard the carriage come slowly to the front door. She was not far enough dressed yet to lean out and look at it and she grew flustered, thinking she might be late after all. But the others were not quite ready; she heard voices calling in the house and Nell's footsteps running along the gallery. Someone had made a joke, and Nell was laughing. Then the waiting horses stamped and jingled their bits.

Laura jerked back her head and stood rigid listening. This had happened before. Her dream was coming true. She knew it so certainly that her brain cleared in a flash and she saw the carriage waiting, herself in her bedroom and Nell down in the hall as plain as a set of little photographs, while a clock ticked in her ears to mark the minutes she had to spend. She scrambled into a dress, fastened a few of the hooks, and with her hair still flying ran to the door and along the corridor and halfway down the stairs. Nell, smart and pretty, was standing alone in the hall. She looked up at the sound of steps.

'Oh Nell, Nell, my dream is coming true.'

'What do you mean, Lolly? What's the matter?'

'You mustn't go for this drive. Say you won't go.' Laura leant over the banisters to peer in her sister's face.

'Lolly dear, I must go. Don't be silly.'

'You mustn't. Please don't, Nell. Just to please me.'

Nell looked uncomfortable and Laura's brain began to cloud. The photographic clearness vanished and she felt a twinge of uncertainty. Perhaps her dream had meant nothing. Was she being absurd? Just as she hesitated her uncle walked out of his study and stopped astounded in the hall. At the same time Mrs Young came trailing from the drawing room, Birdie appeared at the top of the stairs, and a maid stepped in from the vestibule with the dust-cover on her arm. They stood in a horrified ring gaping at her while she, trembling, dishevelled, bent her tearful face to Nell.

Mr Young spoke first; his voice was harsh with rage. 'What are you doing here, Laura? Control yourself.'

At the ugly note Nell turned and faced him boldly. 'Laura has had a bad dream, Uncle. She wants me to stay at home. I should like to stop with her if you will let me.'

'I shall do nothing of the sort. You are coming for a drive with me.'

'But, Uncle, I don't think Laura ought to be left alone.'

'Nell, you must allow me to do as I think best. I cannot let hysteria upset the whole house. Miss Bird,' he called to the governess hovering on the stairs, 'will you please take Laura with you up to her room and look after her till we come back.'

Birdie came down and put a hand on Laura's arm, but she shook herself free from the hateful touch and rushed upstairs stumbling over the hem of her dress as she went. She was shaken by dry tearing sobs that echoed through the hall; as they broke out she felt Nell turn to run up after her, heard her uncle call her back and just caught the beginning of a violent argument. How it ended she could not tell, because when she got to her bedroom Birdie behind her fumbled at the door, then clapped it to and locked it from the outside, afterwards shutting the double doors into the gallery. Then she went into their sitting room and tinkled glasses in the medicine cupboard. Laura flung herself on her bedroom door, tried the handle, and then began to drum with her fists on the wood. Presently she heard another hammering outside: someone was knocking on the outer door. It must have been Nell, for Birdie cried 'I won't let you in.' The handle rattled once or twice, then all was still.

Laura sank down in the corner by the door crying, a weak pitiful crying in her longing for Nell. She had failed, she told herself, by being weak; if only she had been firm enough Nell might have been saved from the drive. She strained her ears for sounds from the waiting carriage; at any minute now her sister would leave the house. And as she listened she suddenly heard a scraping at the window and looked up to see Nell's face peeping in. Nell was nodding and grinning with pride at her own daring but her wide open eyes showed that she was a little afraid. Laura, helpless, clapped hand to mouth and screamed behind them thinly; in screaming she saw piercingly a new side to her dream. And as she screamed a look of discomfort swept the smiling features, there was a scrambling sound and her sister fell.

Nell had gone into Birdie's room and climbed along the ledge to see Laura, an easy journey till she reached the moulding round the window. Then she had grasped an iron staple while stretching to peer in; it had come out of its socket under her hand. Death was instantaneous, they told Laura. Actually she died when her uncle tried to move her. He was the first to reach her when the servants shouted. The coachman and footman were struggling to hold the horses.

CHAPTER XIII

FROM the spare room where she had slept ever since the accident Laura could see a garden boy weeding the drive. He had been at it for three mornings and he was halfway round the curve; today she meant to catch him as he came from work.

She was getting better. She was still weak and nervous, startled by sudden sounds, easily made cry, but the doctor came less often now, prescribed fewer sleeping draughts and let her do very much as she liked. She got up every day and sat by the window; nobody urged her to go downstairs. Her uncle and aunt kept away from her room: meetings were too painful and reduced her to tears. Birdie sat with her in the afternoons and evenings, often offering to read aloud. Sometimes Laura listened to the reading; more often she followed a train of private thought.

It was not thought exactly, it was rather planning. Thought moves backward and forward along the line of time and Laura dared not let her mind look back. Behind her towered a dark threatening wave; if she turned, it would fall on her. She could only escape by planning for the future, and while she was weak it was difficult even to do this. The business of eating meals and taking medicines, the slow processes of washing and dressing, the doctor's visits, the general solicitous fuss took up so much of her day that she had little time left for herself. If she was quiet for too long Birdie began to talk to her; it was in self-defence that Laura first asked her to read. Then the hours of reading became her refuge; behind the sheltering murmur she made her plans. It surprised her to discover how little Birdie noticed: could she not suspect or even feel the determining, the resolving? Laura felt worn out sometimes from the effort of planning. But what she planned she kept to herself.

One week the doctor had talked of a change of air. Would Miss Young care for Felixstowe? The season was over now and the place would be quiet. A short stay there might do her good.

'What do my uncle and aunt say?'

'They suggested it.'

'I'd like to go away. I don't mind where.'

'The journey to Felixstowe is easy.'

'Very well; I will go there.'

The thought of going away made her energetic. She went up the next morning to her painting room. Birdie followed presently to see what she was doing, but Laura was only sorting old canvases.

And today Birdie was away from Yule Lodge: she had gone to look for lodgings for herself and Laura. Laura was therefore able this morning to get up earlier than usual, and she sat at the window watching the garden boy. Today she could execute her scheme without any fear of interruption. The house would be almost empty in the evening as Mr and Mrs Young were going for a drive. Probably a maid would come and sit with her, but Laura felt strong enough now to send the girl away. She had made up her mind upon every detail when the outside bell rang for the servants' dinner. The boy on the gravel straightened his back, collected his tools in a wheelbarrow and began to trundle them towards the house.

Laura had so often planned how she would creep to the front door that she was halfway downstairs before a strangeness in the hall distressed her – two books now on a table and a new grouping of the ferns. It was more than three weeks since she had last come here. Memory struck her mind as a blow might strike her body. Nell stood for an instant like a physical presence below her, gay and pretty, ready to go for a drive. The illusion was so violent that Laura stopped and shut her eyes. To go on, she felt, would now dishonour the dead. Once she had passed through the hall she could never say, 'Last time I came here I was with Nell,' and she might never again fancy she saw her sister standing there. It would perhaps be better to go round another way.

But to try the backstairs would be to risk discovery; she might meet someone who would thwart her plans. And since these plans would be a greater memorial to Nell, since she meant to change her whole life for her dead sister's sake, she forced herself to confront the pain of her memories and went on down, crossing the hall without once looking up. She passed through the baize doors into the entrance and waited there for the boy to come by. She could not face going out into the porch.

Jack came along trundling the barrow so noisily that Laura thought her call to him was lost in the din. But he had heard her and looked round, setting down the barrow and touching his forelock when he saw who had called.

'Jack, come here. I want to talk to you.'

'Yes, miss.' He was an ugly little boy whom she and Nell rather liked. He was usually so friendly that Laura could not understand the awkwardness of his approach till it struck her that he had never seen her in deep mourning before, and that his embarrassment might spring partly from sympathy.

'What time do you stop work in the evening, Jack?'

'Six o'clock, I reckon to.'

'Will you bring your barrow then to the garden door? I've got some rubbish I want to burn and I can't carry it all.'

'Yes, miss.' He spoke without enthusiasm, ears very red and his face looking down.

'Are you sure you can come? I want to make a bonfire.'

'Yes, miss.'

'Do you know how to make a bonfire, Jack? Could you make it if I gave you the things to burn?'

'Coo, yes; do I get matches.' He lifted his head at last.

'I'll give you matches. It'll be a big fire: I want to burn some pictures. But I don't want anyone to interfere.'

'Right you are, miss.' He went back to his barrow. Evidently a bargain had been made.

Laura's knees shook so much as she went upstairs again that she wondered if she had enough strength to carry her plan through. She made herself rest on the sofa after lunch; Aunt Carrie looked approval when she came in for a little chat.

'We are going for a short drive after tea, my dear. Sarah will come up to see if you want anything.'

Sarah came up and was shocked to find Laura putting on outdoor things. 'Oh Miss Laura, you aren't fit to go out yet. Why, you haven't hardly been downstairs.'

'Indeed I have, Sarah. I've been downstairs and upstairs too. And I'm only going out for a few minutes in the garden.'

'The mistress never said – '

'The mistress didn't know. Now listen, Sarah. There are some things that I don't want to see again when I come back from Felixstowe – things that would make me unhappy if I found them in the house. I want to burn them before I go and I want to burn them when there's nobody about. They are pictures; you must help me get them down from upstairs.'

'I'll burn them for you, Miss Laura, if you'll tell me what.'

'No, I want to do it myself. Jack is coming with a barrow to the garden door.'

Jack's coming with a barrow reassured Sarah. An arrangement so definite seemed more than mere caprice. She carried the pictures down at last and stacked them in the barrow; they were hard to pile as Laura had left them stretched, not knowing if the canvas would burn without the wooden frames. Jack in assuming charge of the load wedged Margaret's portrait tightly. He scraped it against the side of the barrow, and when Laura saw the marks on the paint she caught her breath in a curious anguish that pleased as keenly as it hurt. 'Bind the sacrifice with cords, yea, even to the horns of the altar.' From some scripture lesson of Birdie's the words came back to her. She clenched her teeth to prevent herself chanting them aloud. Sarah glanced at her, clacked her tongue at the boy and then seemed prepared to follow them both.

'Sarah, please wait indoors and fetch me at once if the carriage comes.'

'Oh Miss Laura, are you sure you can manage?'

'Quite well, thank you. Jack will look after me.'

The boy took up the handles briskly and set off through the shrubbery. Laura had chosen her hour well: the other gardeners had gone home and there was nobody but Jack to protest when she ordered him not to go to the rubbish heap but to the wood beyond the kitchen garden wall.

'Keeper won't like us going in there.'

'We shan't go far in.'

He trundled the barrow through the fringe of nettles, shut the door on the daring act and looked round for orders. 'I've brought paper and there are plenty of dry sticks,' said Laura. 'We'll burn the pictures one by one.'

Jack grew excited as he rushed about collecting sticks and he soon had enough for a big fire. His fingers trembled as he struck the first match and lit the paper. Then he blew vigorously till the heap was ablaze. When Laura took the first picture off the barrow he snatched it from her and balanced it on the pile. In a second the paint began to burn; then with a roar the whole burst into flame. Intoxication seized Jack. With his nose and eyes running he swung up a great bough and dug it into the fire. As Laura threw on picture after picture he jumped and screamed like a mad creature and jabbed the surfaces, yelling with gusto 'Hark at 'n sizzling,' 'Coo, that's done.' He slashed at the huge portrait of Margaret till he knocked the fire to pieces; but Laura shouted at him and he scampered off to get more boughs.

Laura herself stood poking the blaze with a stick, standing as near to it as she could. Her head began to swim and she felt her body swaying, but the pain as her pictures burned filled her with ecstasy; never before had she found such delight in pain. Jack's shouts, the roar and heat of the fire, the thick rolling up of the smoke between the trees, made a wild scene in which nothing had reality but the canvases she was throwing away. Each as she lifted it seemed solid and familiar. Each met her eyes in a sort of appeal – and with dreadful satisfaction she ignored the appeal and threw the picture into the flames.

Presently she remembered she had something else to burn and when Jack next ran off she took a letter out of her pocket, tore it across and tossed it in. The fire was low by now and devoured the pages slowly; they turned grey and brittle but kept their shape and on the metallic surfaces some of the words showed plain. 'Ever,' cried Chloe's square handwriting from the bonfire. 'Ever,' chanted Laura and ground the sheets to ash.

The door in the wall creaked open, then shut with a bang, and Jack became a well-behaved boy again. All the canvases had been burnt and the fire was dying down. The hour of delirium was over.

Laura blinking in the heat could not see the intruding figure until Margaret Fraser came timidly out from the shadow of the wall. They had not met since the day of Miss Forncett's visit and Laura felt irritated. If Margaret was too shy to come after the accident what was the good of coming now? And, coming at all, why not come boldly? What help was there in this furtive advance? To break with Margaret Fraser had been part of Laura's plan; she had worded several dignified letters to her in her head. But as the girl came nearer, a mood of cruelty suddenly seized Laura, and she resolved to be rid of her at once. She pushed a stick into the fire and stared with hostile eyes. She could frighten Margaret with the stick – yes, wave it burning in her face and singe her hair. She felt that Jack was expecting her to do just this and that Margaret was half afraid she might. The apprehension in their faces gave their thoughts away. They believed her mad; well, then, she could behave as she liked.

'Why didn't you come before?' she said at last.

'Oh Laura, I didn't like to. Father said "Why don't you go" but I thought it better to wait a bit.'

'Well, you're too late now. I am going away.'

'I know; they told me at the house. I have come to say goodbye, I shall be gone to College before you are back.'

'It's goodbye for ever then. I am not coming back.'

'Why, Laura, what are you going to do?'

'Never mind. I have made my plans.'

'But you will write to me? I shall always write to you.'

'What is the good? We shall never meet again.'

Tears sprang into Margaret's eyes. She looked so soft and weak that Laura in contempt went on: 'Besides, I don't want to write. Our friendship is over.'

'Laura, why? What have I done?'

'Oh, you've done nothing. It's I who am changing my ways.'

'I don't understand,' began Margaret, then gulped and blew her nose. Laura stirred the fire and took no notice. She was wondering how long it would take to drive the girl away, but Margaret recovered her voice and ventured another remark.

'Chloe asked me to give you her love.'

'Thank you. Please remember me to her. She, I think, will understand.'

Margaret winced at Laura's tone. This last thrust was too much.

'Well, goodbye,' she said, holding out her hand.

Laura swept her branch out of the fire with a flourish. Sparks flew, Margaret backed, and Jack rushed to the door. He lifted the barrow up and turned it round for flight. What would happen next? He stared at the girls with enormous eyes.

'Jack will take you out,' called Laura, flinging back her head in her disdain. 'You are as frightened as he is. Please go with him.' She swung the branch to and fro over the fire, scattering ash and raising in the draught a few last thin flames that blew backwards and forwards. It was impossible for Margaret to come round to her, so after hesitating a little longer she turned to Jack, who pushed the barrow towards the door in evident relief.

'Jack, leave me your rake,' called Laura just at the last

moment. 'I shall want it to rake out all this burned stuff.' The boy ran up with it and Laura took it, turned her back on Margaret and never looked round till the door had banged again and she knew she was alone. Then for some reason she began to cry, but as she cried she raked and trod on the embers till by degrees she had got them black. When the boy came back the fire was out.

CHAPTER XIV

'WHY, I do believe ...' said Birdie in great excitement, 'Yes, it is, Laura. There's Mr Armstrong.'

'Where is he?' Laura leant forward in her chair and stared along the promenade.

'There – just beyond those children. Can he be looking for us?'

'I'm sure he is. I wrote and asked him to come. Birdie, will you go and fetch him. Then he can sit with me while you do your shopping.'

'Are you warm enough, my dear? There's a nip in the air today.'

'Oh yes, I'm hot. Please hurry, or you'll miss him.'

Birdie pushed her knitting into the basket with her purse and the books from Mudie's Library and bustled after Henry like a consequential bee. She attracted his attention after two vain efforts. A certain amount of gesticulation followed, and then Henry came striding up to look for Laura. His face puckered with sorrow as he saw her in her black dress and he took the chair beside her very gently indeed, as if she were some rare bird that he did not want to startle. Then he looked at her again but could find nothing to say and sat a little stiffly waiting for her to speak.

'What did Birdie tell you just now about me?'

'She said you were better.' Then he added, 'Is that true?'

'Oh yes; in some ways I am well again.'

'And in other ways – ?'

'Henry, I want advice.'

'I thought perhaps that was why you wrote. I am glad you did.'

'It is good of you to come so soon.'

'Soon? Why, I would have come when I got your letter yesterday, but I had an appointment at the India Office that I couldn't put off.'

There was another silence. Laura felt at a loss. Her plans were ready, but she did not know how to begin. Henry felt her embarrassment and so went on talking.

'Are you quite comfortable here in your rooms?'

'Oh yes, I think so.'

'You don't want to hurry back to Yule?'

'No. Oh Henry, you've guessed what I want to talk about. I don't want to go back to Yule again.'

'You mean never?'

'Not to my dying day. Never, never.'

He gave a guarded look at her excited face. Laura jerked her head from him with a strange feeling of treachery, stared out to sea and said deliberately, 'What shall I do? What can I do? Is there any way to avoid going back?'

A long silence followed. Henry crossed his legs and stared at the tip of his boot. Twice he drew his breath to speak, but no words came. Then very simply and without effort he said, 'There is one way, Laura, of course. A way I should like.'

He turned and saw self-consciousness in her face.

'Your aunt has spoken to you of this.'

Laura nodded.

'What did she tell you?'

'She thought you wanted Nell.' Her voice trembled at the name.

'But you knew better?'

Again she nodded.

'And you sent for me.' A great joy lit his face. Its unexpected intensity made her ashamed, and with a harsh, 'Henry, no,' she snatched her hands from her lap as sharply as if he had moved his own towards them.

There was a short uncomfortable silence. Then, 'Laura,

what do you really want?' said Henry sternly.

His anger was invigorating. She loved him for it. Here was someone to whom she could tell the truth. Something loosened in her mind, a barrier broke down, and on a wave of emotion she began to speak, almost sobbing in the relief of having someone to talk to, of being free from the pressure she had felt for so long.

'Henry,' she said quickly, 'please don't look at me; please keep your head turned away. For I am ashamed of myself and before I tell you anything more I must beg your pardon very humbly for being so selfish. Oh,' she added, turning to him and quite forgetting she had told him not to look, 'all my life I have thought only of myself. How can one learn to be unselfish?'

'Well, get on with your story, Lolly.'

'Do you remember when you stayed with us in July I told you about my dream? I said it would be my fault if the dream came true and you said I mustn't let myself be frightened.'

'I remember it very well.'

'You see, we were both right. The dream came true, and it was my fault for being frightened.'

Her voice shook and she stopped to control herself. He gave her a moment and then ventured, 'Would it be too much for you to tell me what happened? I never heard a connected story. You were shut up in your room and Nell climbed along the ledge to look at you. Was it a joke or was she unhappy about you? And in either case how could the accident be your fault?'

'You make events sound too simple; they were dreadfully complicated. After you left the Lodge everything went wrong. I managed to offend everybody in the house; I was so tiresome that finally I made Uncle very angry and the day before the accident he gave me a terrible scolding. That night I had horrible dreams and the next day I felt ill and was lying down while the others were dressing to go out in the new carriage. And suddenly Nell laughed and the horses jingled their bits exactly as I had heard them in my first dream. I thought Nell was in danger and I ran down to stop her going for the drive. Of course I seemed crazy – you would have thought so too. I had no time to put up my hair or to look tidy. Uncle said I was hysterical and sent me upstairs with Miss Bird. Nell thought they were being unkind to me and as she couldn't get at me any other way she climbed along the ledge to look at me. And when I saw her at the window I knew what I had done. In fussing over her I had forgotten to guard her against myself. It was from me all the time that the danger came. If I had behaved better she need never have come along the ledge.'

She began to sob openly. He put his arm along the back of her chair and sat a little forward to give her shelter. This was the first time she had cried for Nell in the presence of another person; the gushing of her tears gave her relief. Crying seemed less bitter with Henry beside her. He did not touch her or try to console her and even in her distress she felt grateful to him. He was the gentlest, the most patient person she had ever known. Then her gratitude reminded her that she owed him some more explanations. Time was passing and Birdie would soon be back. She choked back her tears, sat up and straightened her hat, then looked round and began to wipe her eyes. A woman sitting near them was staring inquisitively, and Laura glanced in some alarm at Henry. He met her look with undisturbed tenderness; her crying in public did not seem to embarrass him.

'Poor little Lolly! So all this has been on your mind ever since?'

'Yes. When I was ill I thought it all through. I began at the beginning when we first came to the house and I saw that whenever Uncle had wanted one thing I wanted something else. He hoped we should be happy in the life he had planned; all I thought about was my painting.'

'Well, is it not important to you?'

'Yes; but then Nell's music was important to her and yet she did not let it interfere with the rest of her life. She has always been more unselfish than I am; she liked pleasing people, you understand. And I could perhaps please people too if I paid less attention to my own affairs.'

Henry only grunted and Laura went on, 'At first when I thought about Nell I felt I would like to die too, but presently I saw that this was cowardly, not enough of a punishment. It would be better to make my life a sort of memorial to Nell, and the best memorial would be to change myself. So as a beginning I burned my pictures; they were at the root of the trouble, you see.'

She felt his disapproval. 'Was that necessary?'

'Yes, I had to.'

'Very well. And then?'

'Oh Henry, I felt so lonely. You can't think how queer it was with my pictures gone. I knew I ought to go on living at Yule and being grateful for Uncle's kindness, but I couldn't. I was, I still am, frightened of him. I can't stay there without Nell to protect me.' Already she had strayed a little from the truth, now she faltered reddening at the edge of dangerous ground. It was impossible to tell him more. But Henry saw at once where the story led.

'So you wanted a guardian and sent for me. Am I to be part of your punishment, Lolly?'

She had never heard his voice so harsh. Tears came into her eyes. She blinked them away and floundered on in clumsy sentences. 'I beg your pardon, Henry. I never thought – I meant it to be a sort of arrangement. I didn't know you – ' she broke off crimsoning to the roots of her hair as she saw she had embarrassed him.

They sat side by side in acute discomfort. Laura longed to get up and run away, but Birdie had tucked the rugs round her so securely that she could not leave her chair without a struggle and she felt much too frightened to make the attempt.

Henry recovered and said rather sadly, 'Lolly, I'm afraid you're a baby still.'

Meekly Lolly agreed she was.

'Listen,' he went on without turning his head. He had

shifted away from her in his chair. 'Suppose I said that I should be proud if just as an arrangement, as you call it, we should go on with your plan. Then I should have the right to look after you and perhaps if we waited the rest might come.'

In a flash Laura had her answer ready; in that flash she saw what she had learned. He was offering what she had planned for herself. Here was the new life, here the new Lolly might emerge: a woman rejecting the dangerous joys that make one self-absorbed, devoted to her husband, living for him. If this woman emerged, Nell had not died in vain: such a life would be a true memorial to her. But the last few minutes had taught Laura that the scheme was childish, a phantasy taken from one of Birdie's Sunday reading books. Its only reality was its convenience. If she married Henry she might leave Yule for ever and begin a new life in security. And in addition she was wanted; he was willing to make the unequal bargain. That an acceptance should be convenient filled her with shame; she turned to him with fierce affection.

'No, no,' she cried, 'we musn't take the risk. The best thing we have between us is a sort of confidence. You are the only person in the world to whom I can tell the truth. If I married you like this, unequally, I should always be shy of you. If the plan went wrong I should be afraid to tell you and in the end we might lose honesty without gaining anything more.'

'There is the difference in age,' he sighed.

'It's not that, Henry. That wouldn't matter. It's just that I don't want to marry anybody. I don't think I'm ready to marry yet.' Then seeing him still unsatisfied she added earnestly, 'Please forgive me for bringing you here for nothing. Yet I feel much happier, as I always do when I have talked to you.'

Whatever regret was in his mind had cleared from his face by the time he looked at her. 'Well, that is something at least, Lolly. Bless you for saying it. And why should I have come for nothing? I'll try to be useful at least.'

He stood up and took her hand. Birdie had come back and

with ostentatious tact was sitting in a shelter a little way off.

'Let me go now, my dear, I have a scheme in my head, but I can think it out more impartially alone. Indeed,' he added, 'it will need impartiality, for it is a plan I should very much like. But before I tell you I must consult your uncle and I must also go to London to see my sister. You will be here next week?'

'Oh, yes; we shall stay.'

'Then I'll come back and find you.' And he was gone.

'I didn't know Henry's sister lived in London,' observed Laura to Birdie later in the day. 'I wonder we have never met her.'

'I don't think your dear aunt cares for her.'

'Why not?'

Birdie counting stitches raised her eyebrows and was silent. Laura waited – and then put her question again.

'I don't think Mrs Young approves of the way she behaved.'

'What did she do?'

'She ran away from her husband.'

'Perhaps he was unkind to her?'

A sniff from Birdie. She sniffed however more to uphold the general sanctity of marriage than to express disapproval of a particular case. For when Laura plied her with further questions Birdie had to confess that she knew almost nothing of the story.

Laura spent the next few days in deep tranquillity. Her plan had failed, she had refused to marry Henry. The memorial to Nell was taking a different shape. Yet she felt neither remorse nor shame, only the comfort of a great relief. She was as tired as if she had been carrying a load, as free as if she had put it down. At night she slept so soundly that morning came in a flash; by day she seemed to doze in quiet content.

Birdie found her so untroubled that she ventured to leave her and pay morning visits to a dressmaker. Luckily an excellent woman had rooms on the front; during fittings

Birdie could keep an eye on her charge. If Laura simply waved a hand, help would come at once.

'But, Birdie, you couldn't rush out to me if you weren't properly dressed.'

'If the worst came to the worst, my dear, I should sent the apprentice.'

'Well, I don't think you need be afraid. I shall be quite happy by myself.'

'If the worst came to the worst, my dear, I should send the

Birdie, with more protestations, went off to her dressmaker. Laura hardly noticed when she went or came; the little woman had no power to tease her now. The absorbing hours of fitting grew long and longer, but Laura had no sense of loneliness. She basked in the sunshine on the front, sometimes sketching on bits of notepaper. More often she sat staring out where haze tricked judgment and the fishing boats seemed to hang in a gap between sea and sky. She fancied herself like one of those fishing boats, in tranquil suspense between realities. All her past life had closed like a dream, even grief for Nell was temporarily numb. And fear of the future no longer distressed her: Henry had said he would think out a scheme.

He came back within a week and they met without shyness: their last interview had given them ease. Birdie was in the town; Laura was sitting alone; and he came striding up as he did before and took a chair. He was slow to speak as usual but seemed pleased with himself; there was almost a jauntiness in his look.

'Well, Henry?'

He turned to her beaming. 'Laura, you must be honest; tell me at once if you dislike the plan. I find I cannot think of it impartially: it is something I should like so much.'

'Go on, go on.'

'You know, perhaps, that my sister lives in London. I ought first to tell you about her, I think. She is ten years older than I am, a widow, not at all likely to marry again – she is too busy enjoying all sorts of activities. But she has no children, and she is sometimes lonely; if you would care to go and stay with her she would be very glad to have you.'

Laura considered the statements one by one. 'What do they say at Yule?' she asked at length.

'They will consent if you wish it. I must warn you that Mrs Young has never approved of Marian, but both she and your uncle believe you might be happy with her in London.'

'Tell me more about your sister. What is she like?'

'To look at, you mean?'

'I didn't really. Still, perhaps it would be best to begin with her looks.'

Henry seemed to search his memory. 'I don't know what to tell you. There's nothing to describe. Oh yes, she talks a great deal.'

'That's not a description of her face.'

'Well, she has a good face. At least, I think so.'

'A good face?'

'Yes. Good features, I think; the sort of face you can trust. But she also looks like a person who knows what she wants and gets it.'

'Does she always get it?'

'Now she does. She used not to.'

He clasped his hands and leant forward with his elbows on his knees. Something important was coming, Laura knew.

'She has not had a happy life. She was married when she was quite young. My father was a selfish old fellow and he let her make a foolish match. Not socially, you understand, but in every other way. She made the best of it for a number of years but at last she left her husband and went to live with an elderly cousin of ours. Perhaps it was not a wise choice but she had to find some sort of refuge. My father was dead by then, I was in India, and Marian has never got on with my elder brother. Cousin Charlotte was rich, rather eccentric, and devoted to Marian. She made a great fuss of her, took her about, and scandalised the people who think that a wife living apart from her husband ought not to be cheerful. Anyway, so many spiteful things were said in London that they lived a great deal abroad. They enjoyed travelling and unconventional ways. Then Charlotte died and left her money in trust for Marian, and now that her husband is dead she is a rich widow and people who were once most unkind are beginning to know her again. I get angry when I meet them but she is only amused at the change.'

'Would she like me if I went to her? I am sure I should be shy.'

'Shyness won't matter to Marion.' He began to smile at some recollection. 'She is very kind but you may think her odd. She is taken up with all sorts of schemes, women's suffrage and that sort of thing. Perhaps you may find her too vehement. She seems to hope you will be energetic too; she was asking me about your painting.'

'Is she interested?'

'She paints herself. An extraordinary French style I don't understand. She says it's important; she will talk to you about it. I warn you, Lolly, she will talk and talk.'

'And I may stay for a long time?'

'You may make a home with her.' They both sat silent, weighing these words. Then Henry turned to look at her.

'Laura,' he hesitated. She glanced up. 'Laura, when you feel you can, you ought to go to Yule. Just for a visit, perhaps, to please them there. They are glad you should have a change, but I know they will miss you very much.'

Fearful of hurting her he went on quickly, 'Then you approve, Lolly, of my plan?'

'It is an alarming one. But I'd like to try it.'

'Good. Marian is looking forward to having you.'

'May I go straight to her without going home?'

'She is expecting you as soon as you like. Perhaps Miss Bird could go to settle you in.'

A thought struck Laura. 'Henry, what about you?'

'I sail at the end of the week.'

'What, so soon?' she cried in distress, realizing suddenly that she would miss him.

He went on talking as if silence were dangerous. 'I shall go back to India content to think of you with Marian. I imagine you will be happy in London, busy and amused. You will meet all sorts of people.'

He stopped abruptly and she heard him swallow. He had something difficult to say.

'And Laura, if you meet some sensible young fellow of the proper age whom Marian likes and your uncle approves of – well, I suppose if you want to you must marry him. But if there's nobody when I come back in two years' time – ' He jerked up his chin and turned to her almost fiercely, stern eyes under the furious brows. 'But mind, you're not in any way to consider yourself bound. For all you know I may marry a native woman yet. We're neither of us tied in the least, d'you understand?'

Half laughing, half crying, she met his look.

'But you might let me know how you get on. I think I have the right to demand an occasional letter, Lolly.'

It was lunch time. People were strolling to their houses. Far off in the distance a siren sounded and a gong, very soft and clear, rang from somewhere near at hand. Birdie was coming towards them with her parcels; behind her stretched a deserted promenade. Suspense was over, the new life had begun. Laura was still too bewildered to know how much she owed him, but a sense of his generosity pierced her through. With a great rush of gratitude she held out her hands. 'Of course, of course I shall write to you – often. You don't know how much I shall want to write.'

EPILOGUE

THE official goodbyes, Indian and European, were over. Henry turned for a last word with the district doctor.

'Well,' the latter grumbled for perhaps the twentieth time, 'we shall miss you, Armstrong. God knows how the place will do under this new fellow.' Henry's going had by now become a grievance with him; he saw in it a sort of treachery.

'Don't depress the man when he's just off,' said his wife. 'And likely to get married as soon as he arrives in England.'

She was a tiresome woman, strident in all weathers. How she had found out about Lolly Henry never knew. By now he loathed her for her persistent teasing; yet he felt too tired to be glad he would never see her again. The interminable leave-taking at last was over. He climbed into the bullock cart for the first stage of the journey.

As the cart creaked away in the dust he realized again his immense fatigue. These last years in the district had worn him out. He lay back like a sack being jolted across country, a lump insentient of discomfort or heat. When the irritations of departure had faded from his mind no other emotion pierced the blank. The thought of leave could not stir his apathy; his feeling, if any, was of dread. Eight hours later he looked at himself in the glass of the station waiting room; his face, washed clean of dust, was lined and haggard, his hair had faded to a tired-looking pepper and salt. An ugly fellow, middle-aged, he told himself savagely.

When he reached Bombay he found his home boat more than usually crowded with women and children. Their presence filled him with a nervous misery, and he avoided them as much as he could. But in the ship's restricted space it was hard to escape them. Their light voices seemed to be continually in earshot. He felt older and lonelier than ever, and the longing for Lolly, lately only a pang, became a misery that would not let him sleep.

They had a good voyage, reaching Marseilles a day ahead of the scheduled time. A couple of subalterns made a dash with him for an earlier train. They were well-mannered boys who deferred to him and called him 'sir'. They would be the right age for Lolly, he supposed, and he envied them their assurance and gaiety.

He reached his sister's house soon after lunch on a fine mid-May afternoon. His telegram had miscarried and he was not expected so soon. Both ladies were out but his room was ready. He was glad enough of a bath and a change.

Afterwards he must have dozed in a chair by the window. He woke with a guilty start at the sound of a gong and went downstairs feeling extraordinarily refreshed and a little light-headed, as if he were moving in a dream.

Marian was waiting in the drawing room, handsomer than ever now that her hair was white. They kissed each other with genuine affection, but Henry's heart sank when he saw they were having tea alone. He knew his sister's determination and he did not feel ready to talk about Laura yet.

'Henry, you look tired out,' she exclaimed, as he took a chair beside her. 'Thank goodness you've left that dreadful district. Did you have a very tiresome journey home?'

'Not too bad,' he said, reflecting that he could remember nothing of it but his longing for Lolly. And he hastily ate bread and butter to prevent himself talking about her.

Marian spoke of other things for a little, then looked at him directly and began, 'I suppose you know your Lolly has become an extremely sought after young woman?'

'My Lolly?'

'Well, why not? I imagine there is nobody else, though the young woman is reserved and keeps her own counsels. I did as you told me, my dear,' she went on, as if in answer to an unspoken question, 'I introduced her to all and sundry. You may have gathered from my letters that I spared no effort.' Her black eyes twinkled as she thought of all she had done. 'My heart has often been in my mouth, I assure you. I saw myself getting into hot water all round. There was a young Italian, a son of friends of mine in Rome – goodness knows what the Youngs would have thought of him. However, that passed off; I was much relieved. And I'm very glad you're back, Henry. I don't want any young whippersnapper to get her. As you know, I've never thought much of the young of either sex, and it sometimes seems to me that present-day youth is shallower, more selfish, than ever before. Not one of Lolly's admirers is fit to hold a candle to her. She must go to someone who can appreciate her qualities.'

He looked away from her and stirred uneasily. Marian always went too fast for him. The matter was not as simple as she seemed to think; had she no idea what he was feeling? To meet Lolly in her presence had become intolerable now; he searched the room for a way of escape.

'Where is she, by the way?' he grumbled at last, as if he felt affronted by her absence.

'Oh, classes in York Place this afternoon. Philosophy, I believe,' said Marian with a comic look. 'Henry, why don't you go and meet her? The College is only a quarter of an hour's walk away and she will be out at five.'

'I think I will,' he said, with immense relief. It would be so much easier to meet her out of doors, out of Marian's sight. As he looked for his hat in the hall he found a stick; he took it with him with a vague hope that it would encourage him.

London looked beautiful this afternoon – pink and white may trees in the squares, the window boxes gay. In this sedate quarter the distant cries and roll of traffic made no more than a murmurous background. A water cart preceding him filled the streets with freshness. A leisurely carriage passed with a mother and daughter inside, their parasols slanted over dazzling finery. Henry gazed in horror at the latest fashion in hats. How could women allow themselves to look so absurd?

The hats had so startled him that he began to hurry and reached the College much too soon. A cab was drawn up at the door and two maidservants stood on the pavement waiting for their charges. Henry sauntered slowly up the shady side of the street, wondering if he ought to cross and enquire for Miss Young. Were men allowed inside a Women's College? He felt extremely helpless and rather ill at ease.

He tried to imagine what Laura would look like when she emerged, but for all his excitement he could not picture her. He remembered that she had very beautiful eyebrows and that one could read her wishes from them. But the rest of her features escaped his search, he could only see her as a long-ago figure – an excited child running races with Nell, a white-faced girl on the front at Felixstowe. At the thought of Felixstowe his pulse began to race; that occasion had been one of the hardest in his life. He tried to calm himself again by looking at his watch. He would walk up the street and then back down it and turn again to meet her just as she left the door. She would certainly be late, he must not expect her too soon; he forced himself to walk on for two hundred paces. As a result he had no time for any manoeuvres. When he turned round and came back again the pupils were already leaving the College; two girls with their hair down their backs set off with their chaperones. Another couple came out and got into the carriage; several more hurried off as he came up. The open door by now was a humming centre of activity. Henry kept well away from it on the far side of the street.

Then he saw her. A knot of girls had come trooping on to the pavement, Laura in the middle surrounded by a chattering crowd. She was wearing just such a little hat as the elegant girl in the carriage had been wearing, and he saw how enchanting the fashion was for the right sort of face. And he saw that Laura's companions also found her enchanting. 'Laura,' 'Miss Young,' 'Dearest Miss Young,' buzzed half a dozen voices. Henry listening cursed himself for a fool. Now he must in some way attract her attention. What would she think when she saw him waiting in the street like this? How embarrassing for her to be watched by all these girls, or indeed by the grey-haired woman who had come out on the portico of the College and was peering down to see why so much noise went on below.

Then, as he hesitated, miserably undecided, she looked across and saw him. How she managed it he did not know, but the girls vanished, she came straight across, they turned a corner together and were alone in a quiet street. He took her books from her and looked at her but did not dare to speak. Indeed, he did not trust his voice. He had thought she could never change, he was wrong: she could grow lovelier. The miracle walking beside him took his breath away. Here was all he had ever adored grown grander, richer; Lolly the difficult girl a magic woman. Jealousy shook him as he thought of her London years. What had she learned to become so glorious?

He must explain that he had only come to see, that he was going away again immediately, that she must, that she must – he cleared his throat half a dozen times but nothing happened and he walked on in desperation beside her, waving his stick awkwardly and twisting his face in his effort to begin.

At last Lolly stood still and began to laugh. The little wretch, she had learned to laugh at him. They were crossing by the railings of a quiet square. Sparrows were pecking oats in the gutter beside them, the trees in the square hung over them brilliant green. Laura stopped to open her parasol before going on into the sunlight. As she fiddled with the catch she raised her face to him.

'Are you trying to tell me you've married a native woman, Henry?'

He looked at her full in the eyes and found all he had ever found there, Laura's wise little guarded look with its humour and tenderness. And then he found something beyond that: an anticipation, a flash, that raised a hammering in his heart. 'Why, Lolly – ' he cried, he did more than cry, he shouted.

The sparrows flew away in a startled cloud, a woman pulling a distant door bell turned her head.

But after the cry he could say no more. Still with the cane at a ridiculous angle he stared an amazed enquiry into her face. His own was transfigured but incredulous. Then Laura left her tiresome parasol unopened and for further answer put her hand in his.